The Shadow Was Less Than Fifty Feet Away. . . .

With a frantic movement, Cargill pulled the girl out of the chair, settled into it and grabbed the gun. A sheet of flame reared up a dozen feet in front of the Shadow.

The flame glazed through the Shadow. Behind him grass and shrubbery burned with a white intensity. Twice more Cargill fired directly into the Shadow shape—and each time it was as if there was nothing there, no resistance, no substance. And the Shadow came closer. Cargill ceased firing. He was trembling. There was a thought in his mind—a new, overpowering thought. If the Shadow shape were insubstantial, if potent, palpable energy meant nothing to it, then what about steel walls?

The next instant he had his answer. There was a blur of movement near the door, a swelling darkness. Lela screamed.

And then the Shadow was in the room. . . .

Books by A. E. van Vogt

The Mind Cage
Mission to the Stars
Renaissance
The Universe Maker
The Violent Man
The Weapon Makers
The Weapon Shops of Isher

Published by POCKET BOOKS

THE UNIVERSE MAKER

A. E. van Vogt

PUBLISHED BY POCKET BOOKS NEW YORK

POCKET BOOKS, a Simon & Schuster division of
GULF & WESTERN CORPORATION
1230 Avenue of the Americas, New York, N.Y. 10020

ISBN: 0-671-83145-3

First Pocket Books printing December, 1979

10 9 8 7 6 5 4 3 2 1

Trademarks registered in the United States and other countries.

Printed in the U.S.A.

1

Lieutenant Morton Cargill staggered as he came out of
the cocktail bar. He stopped and turned, instinctively
seeking support, when he saw a girl emerge from the
same bar. She half fell against him.

They clung to each other, maintaining a precarious
balance. She seemed to recover first. She mumbled,
"'Member, you promised to drive me home."

"Huh?" said Cargill. He was about to add, "Why,
I've never seen you before." He didn't say it because it
suddenly struck him that he had never before in his life
been so drunk either. And there was a vagueness about
the last hour that lent plausibility to her words.

He certainly had intended to find himself a girl before
the evening was over. Besides, what did it matter anyway? This was 1953. He was a man who had three days
left of his embarkation leave and he couldn't stop to
argue about the extent of their acquaintance.

"Where's your car?"

She led the way, weaving, to a Chevrolet coupe. She
let him help her unlock the door. Then she collapsed
onto the seat beside the steering wheel, her head hang-

ing limply. Cargill climbed behind the wheel and almost slid to the floor.

For a moment he pulled himself out of his own blur. He thought, startled, "I'm not fit to drive a car either. I'd better get a taxi."

The impulse faded. As of right now the pickup was a fact—whatever its history—and he was just drunk enough not to have any qualms. He stepped on the starter.

After the crash, Cargill made the first effort to get out of the car. The door wouldn't open. His attempt to move made him aware of how squeezed in he was. Dazed, he realized that only by a miracle had he escaped death and injury.

He tried to reach the door on the other side of the girl. He received his second big shock. The whole front of the car was staved in.

Even in the half darkness Cargill realized that the blow had been mortal to her. Dismayed, he made a new effort to open his own door. This time it worked. He staggered out and off into the darkness. No one tried to stop him. The street seemed deserted.

In the morning, pale and sober, he read the newspaper report of the accident:

GIRL'S BODY FOUND IN WRECK

Her car smashed beyond repair when it sideswiped a tree, Mrs. Marie Chanette last night bled to death from injuries sustained in the accident. The body was not discovered until early this morning and it is believed the victim might have been saved had she been found sooner and treated.

Mrs. Chanette, who was separated from her husband recently, is survived by a three-year-old baby girl and a brother, said to be living in New York. Funeral arrangements await word from relatives.

There was no mention of a possible escort. A later edition mentioned that she had been seen talking to a soldier. That paragraph was enlarged upon in the evening paper. By the second morning there was talk of murder in the news columns, and further mention of the soldier. Taking alarm, the wretched Cargill returned gloomily to his camp.

He was relieved a week later when his group was sent to Korea. There a year stretched between him and the impulse that had made him scamper off into the darkness, leaving behind a dying woman. Battle experience soon hardened him against the reality of death for other people and slowly the awful sense of guilt faded. When early in 1954 he returned as a captain to Los Angeles, he felt recovered. He had been home several months when a note arrived for him in the morning mail:

Dear Captain Cargill:

I saw you on the street the other day and I noticed your name was still listed in the phone book. I wonder if you would be so kind as to meet me at the Hotel Gifford tonight (Wednesday) at about 8:30.

Yours in curiosity,
Marie Chanette.

Cargill read the note, puzzled, and for just a moment the name meant nothing to him. Then he remembered. *"But,"* he thought, stunned, *"she never knew my name."*

It required minutes to shake off the chilling sensation that stole along his spine. At first he decided against keeping the appointment, but as evening arrived he knew he couldn't remain away.

"Yours in curiosity!" What did she mean?

It was 8:15 when he entered the foyer of the magnificent Gifford and took up a position beside a pillar from which he could watch the main entrance.

He waited. At 9:30, he retreated, blushing from his fifth attempt to identify Marie Chanette. He hadn't noticed the man behind the column who was talking to the girl. The girl was smiling sweetly now, the secret smile of a woman who has won the double victory of defending her virtue and simultaneously proving that she is still attractive to other men. Her gaze turned fleetingly, knowingly, and touched Cargill's eyes. Then her attention swung back in a proprietary fashion to the young man. She smiled once more, too sweetly. Then she took her escort's arm and moved off with him through a door above which floated a lighted sign that said alluringly, DREAM ROOM.

The high color faded from Cargill's cheeks as he took up his position once more. But his determination was beginning to wane. Being repulsed by five women was too strenuous for any one evening.

A big man moved up beside him. He said softly, "Captain, how about peddling your wares in some other hotel? Your repeated failure is beginning to embarrass the guests. In other words: Move on, bud, move on. And fast."

Cargill stared with a pale intensity at the house detective's smooth face. He was about to slink off when a young woman's voice said clearly, "Have I kept you waiting long, Captain?"

Cargill swung around in glassy-eyed relief. Then he stopped. His brain roared. He mumbled, "You're Marie Chanette."

She was changed but there was no doubt. It was she. Out of the corner of one eye he saw the house detective move off, baffled. And then there was only the girl, and he was staring at her. "It really is you," he said. "Marie Chanette!"

Her name came hard off his tongue, as if the words were pebbles that interfered with his speech. He began to realize how changed she was, how different.

The girl he had picked up the year before had been well dressed but not like this. Now she wore a "hot pink" sari with a fur coat of indeterminable animal lightly held over her shoulders. It was the most glittering coat Cargill had seen since his return to America.

Her clothes ceased to matter. "But you're dead," he wanted to say. "I read the account of your burial."

He didn't say that. Instead he listened as the girl murmured, "Let's go into the bar. We can talk about . . . old times . . . over a drink."

Without pausing Cargill poured down the first drink. Looking questioningly at the girl, he noted that she was watching him with a faint indulgent smile.

"I wondered," she said, "what it would be like to come back and have a drink with a murderer. It's really not very funny, is it?"

Cargill began to gather his defenses. There was something here he didn't understand, a purpose deeper than appeared on the surface. He had seen suppressed hostility too often not to be able to recognize it instantly. This woman was out to hurt him and he had better watch himself. "I don't know what you mean," he said sharply. His voice had a faint snarl in it. "I'm not sure that I even know you."

The woman did not answer immediately. She opened her purse and took out two large photographs. Without a word she tossed them across the table.

For several seconds Cargill focused his unsteady gaze on the prints. Finally his eyes and his mind coordinated. With a gasp he snatched the pictures up.

Each one showed a man in an officer's uniform in the act of climbing out of a badly wrecked car. The detail of the scenes almost stopped Cargill's breath. One of the prints showed the girl pinned by the door on her side. Her face was twisted and blood was streaming down over her eyes. The second print held a full face of the officer, taken on an upward slant from an almost impossible position behind the girl. Both photographs showed the officer's face, and both showed him squeezing out of the partly open door on the driver's side. In each case the face was his own.

Cargill let the prints drop from limp fingers. He stared at the girl with narrowed eyes. "What do you want?" he asked harshly. Then more violently, "Where did you get those pictures?"

The last question galvanized him into action. He snatched the prints as if defending them from her, as if they were the only evidence against him. With tensed fingers he began to rip them into tiny pieces.

"You can keep those," said the girl calmly. "I have the negatives."

Cargill shifted his feet and he must have looked up, for a waiter darted forward and he heard himself ordering drinks. And then the whiskey was back and he was pouring it down his burning throat. He began to think more sanely. If she were alive after all this time, no charge could be brought against him.

He saw that she was fumbling in her purse. She drew forth a glittering cigarette and, putting it in her mouth, took a deep puff, then exhaled a thin cloud of smoke. Without seeming to notice his gaze fastened on the "cigarette," she delved once again into her purse. She withdrew what appeared to be a slightly over-sized calling card. She tossed it across the table at him.

"You will be wondering," she said, "what this is all

about. There, that explains to some extent. Suppose you look at it."

Cargill scarcely heard.

"That cigarette," he said. "You didn't light it."

"Cigarette?" She looked puzzled; then she seemed to understand. She reached once more into her purse and came out with a second cigarette similar to the one she was smoking. She held it out to him.

"It works automatically," she said, "every time you draw on it. Very simple but I'd forgotten they won't be available for a hundred years yet. They are very soothing."

He needed it. The cigarette seemed to be made of some kind of plastic, but the flavor was of pure mild tobacco. Cargill inhaled deeply three times. Then, his nerves steadier, he forgot the uniqueness of the cigarette and picked up the document she had thrown on the table. A luminous print stared up at him:

THE INTER-TIME SOCIETY
FOR PSYCHOLOGICAL ADJUSTMENTS
recommends
READJUSTMENT THERAPEUTICS
for
Captain Morton Cargill
June 5, 1954
CRIME: MURDER
THERAPY: TO BE MURDERED

Cargill felt a sinking sensation and became conscious of darkness gathering over his mind. He was aware of a boogie-woogie record starting to play nearby. Dazed, he shook himself. Through a growing mist he looked at the girl. "This is silly," he muttered. "You're kidding me."

She shook her head. "It isn't me. Once I went to

them it was out of my control. And as for you, the moment you picked up that card you were—"

Her voice retreated into a remote distance. There was night.

The blackness ended, but his vision remained blurred. After he had blinked hard for several seconds the obstruction cleared away. Automatically, he looked around him.

At first, he did not clearly realize that he was no longer in the DREAM ROOM. Although this setting was entirely different, for a moment his mind made a desperate effort to see a similarity. He tried to think of the cocktail bar as having been stripped of its furniture.

The illusion collapsed. He saw that he was sitting in a chair at one end of a tastefully furnished living room. To his left was an open door through which he could see the edge of a bed. The wall directly across from him was a mirror.

Once more he had to make an adjustment. For as he looked into the "mirror" he saw that there was a girl sitting in what would have been the mirror-image of his own chair. It was the girl who had resembled Marie Chanette.

Cargill started to his feet. In two minutes, in a

frenzy of uneasy amazement, he explored the apartment. The door he had seen when his vision first cleared led to a bedroom with attached bathroom. The bathroom had an outside door but it was locked. He realized that the living room wall was not a mirror at all but a window.

Beyond it was a virtual duplicate of the apartment he was in. There were the same living room and the same door leading to another room—Cargill could not see if it were a bedroom, but he presumed that it was. On one wall of the living room was a clock which said: "May 6, 6:22 P.M." It had obviously stopped working a month ago.

He had been moving with a feverish excitement. Now he retreated warily to a chair and sat there, glaring at the girl. He remembered what she had said in the cocktail bar—remembered the card and its deadly threat.

He was still thinking about it when the girl climbed to her feet and came over to the glass barrier. She said something or rather her mouth moved as if in speech. No sound came through. Cargill was galvanized. He leaped up from his chair and yelled, "Where are we?"

The girl shook her head. Baffled, Cargill explored the wall for a possible means of communication. He looked around the room for a telephone. There was none. Not, he reflected presently, angrily, that a phone would do him any good.

In order to use a phone, it was necessary to have a number to call. There was a way, however. Frantically he searched for pencil and paper in the inside breast pocket of his coat. Sighing with relief, he produced the materials. His fingers trembled as he wrote: *Where are we?*

He held the paper against the glass. The girl nodded her understanding and went back to get her purse. Cargill could see her writing in a small notebook; then she was back at the glass barrier. She held up the paper. Cargill read: *I think this is Shadow City.*

That was meaningless. *Where's that?* Cargill wrote.

The girl shrugged and answered, *Somewhere in the future from both your time and mine.*

That calmed him. He had his first conviction that he was dealing with queer people. His eyes narrowed with calculation. Cautiously he considered the potential danger to himself from a cult that put forward such nonsense. The girl was forgotten, and he went back slowly and settled down in the chair.

"They won't dare harm me," he told himself.

Just how it had been worked he couldn't decide. But apparently the family of Marie Chanette had somehow discovered the identity of the man who had been with the girl when she was killed. In the distorted fashion of kinfolk, they blamed him completely for the accident.

He had no sense of guilt, Cargill told himself. And he certainly had no intention of accepting any nonsense from a bunch of neurotic relatives. Anger welled up in him, but now it was directed and no longer was stimulated by fear and confusion. A dozen plans for counteraction sprang full-grown into his mind. He'd break the glass, smash the door that led from the bathroom, break every stick of furniture in the room. These people were going to regret even this tiny action they had taken against him. For the third time, with deliberation now, he climbed to his feet. He was hefting a chair for his first attack when a man's voice spoke at him from the air directly in front of him.

"Morton Cargill, it is my duty to explain to you why you must be killed."

Cargill remained where he was, rigid.

He unfroze as his mind started to work again. Wildly, he looked around him, seeking the hidden speaker from which the voice had come. He assumed that it had been mechanical. He rejected the momentary illusion that the voice had come from mid-air. In vain, his gaze raked the ceiling, the floor, the walls. He was about to explore more thoroughly with his fingers, with his eyes close up, when the voice spoke again, this time almost in his ear.

"It is necessary," it said, "to talk to you in advance, because of the effect on your nervous system."

The meaning scarcely penetrated. He fought against a sense of panic. The voice had come from a point only inches away from his ear and yet there was nothing. No matter which way he turned the room was empty. Still he discovered no sign of any mechanical device— nothing that could have produced the illusion of somebody speaking directly into his ear.

For a third time, the voice spoke, this time from behind him. "You see, Captain Cargill, the important thing in such a therapy as this is that there be a readjustment on the electro-colloidal level of the body. Such changes cannot be artificially induced. Hypnosis is not adequate because no matter how deep the trance, there is a part of the mind which is aware of the illusion. You will readily see what I mean when I say that even in cases of the most profound amnesia you can presently tell the subject that he will remember everything that has happened. The fact that that memory is here, capable of recall under proper stimulus, explains the futility of standard therapies."

This time there was no doubt. The speech was long, and Cargill had time to turn around, time to assure himself that the voice was coming from a point in the air about a foot or so above his head. The discovery shocked some basic point of stability in him. He had released the chair with which he had intended to smash the furniture. Now he snatched it up again. He stood with it clenched in his hands, eyes narrowed, body almost as stiff as the wood of the chair itself, and listened as once more that disembodied voice spoke.

"Only a fact," it said inexorably, "can affect quick and violent changes. It it not enough to imagine that a machine is bearing down upon you at top speed, even if the imagining is accomplished in a state of deep hypnosis. Only when the machine actually rushes at you and the danger is there in concrete fashion before your eyes—only then does doubt end. Only then does every part of the mind and body accept the reality."

Cargill was beginning to lose some of his own doubts. He had his first sharp feeling that this was real. Here were not just a few angry relatives. He let go of the chair, uncertain now. Here was danger, definite, personal, immediate. And that was something that he could face. For more than a year he had been conditioned to a series of reactions when he was threatened —a remorseless alertness and an almost paradoxical combination of keyed-up relaxation.

He said, "What is all this? Where am I?"

That was becoming tremendously important. He needed information now to stabilize himself. This situation was new and different from anything that he had ever experienced before. What was particularly vital was that he had taken the first step necessary to combat a threat: he tentatively accepted the danger as real.

Someone was doing something against him. Whoever it was had enough money to set up these two quarters in this curious fashion. It looked very expensive, and for that reason alone, convincing. From the air, the voice, ignoring his question, continued:

"It would not be enough to tell the descendants of Marie Chanette that you had been killed. The girl has to see the death scene. She has to look down at you after you have been killed. She has to be able to touch your cold flesh and realize the finality of what has happened. Only thus can we assure adjustment on the electro-colloidal level." The voice finished quietly. "But now, I would suggest that you rest awhile. I want you to have time to evaluate my words. You will hear from me once more this evening—prior to the therapy."

Cargill did not accept the finality of the words. For several minutes he asked questions, talking directly at the point from which the voice had come. There was no reply. In the end, grim and determined, he gave up this approach and returned to an earlier, more violent one. For ten minutes he struck against the glass barrier with the chair. The wooden chair creaked and vibrated from each blow, and shattered section by section. However, the glass was not even scratched.

Reluctantly, Cargill accepted its impregnability. He headed for the bathroom and tested the door that led from it. He gave one tug at the knob and his heart sank —the door was made of a hard metal. For an hour he worked on it without once affecting it in any visible fashion.

Finally, he headed for the bedroom and lay down, intending to rest briefly. He must have instantly fallen asleep.

Somebody was shaking him. Cargill came out of the stupor of sleep to the sound of a woman's voice saying urgently in his ear, "Hurry! There's no time to waste. We must leave at once."

He was a man who expected to be murdered, and that was his first memory. He jerked so spasmodically he felt the wrench of muscles.

And then he was sitting up. He was still in the bedroom of the apartment with the glass wall. The girl who was bending over him was a complete stranger. As he looked at her, she stepped back from him and bent over a small machine. He saw her profile: intent now and almost girlish in the anxiety she was feeling. Something must have gone wrong, for she began to swear in a low tone in a most ungirlish fashion. Abruptly, in evident desperation, she looked at him.

"For . . . sake,"—Cargill didn't get the word—"don't just sit there. Come over here and pull on this jigger. We've got to get out of here."

He was a man trying to grasp many things at once. His gaze flicked apprehensively toward the open door. "Sssssssh!" he whispered instinctively.

The girl's eyes followed his gaze. "Don't worry about them . . . yet. But quick now!"

Cargill moved heavily. His mind held him down. Her presence baffled him. He knelt beside her and grew aware of the faint perfume that emanated from her body. It gave him a heady sensation. For a moment, the tiny pin she was tugging at wavered in his vision. And then once more the girl spoke:

"Grab it," she said, "and pull hard."

Cargill sat there. The expression on his face must have penetrated to her at last for she paused and looked at him hard.

"Oh, mud," she said—it sounded like "mud"—"tell mother all about it. What's eating you?"

He couldn't help it. His mind was twisting, turning, writhing with doubts and fears. "Who are you?" he mumbled.

The girl sagged back. "I get it," she said. "Everything's too fast. You haven't had time to think. You poor little grud you." It sounded like "grud." She shrugged. "Fine, we'll stay here until one of the Shadows comes."

"The what?"

The girl moaned. "Won't I ever learn to keep my mouth shut? I've started him off again."

Her tone cut him at last. A flush touched his cheeks.

He said harshly: "What's all this about? What are you doing here? What—"

The girl held up one hand as if to defend herself from attack. "All right, all right," she said. "I give up. Let's sit down and have a cozy chat, shall we? My name is Ann Reece. I was born twenty-four years ago in a hospital. I spent my first year more or less lying on my back. Then—"

The anger she aroused in him acted like an astringent. It tightened his thoughts and pulled back a dozen wandering impulses into a sort of unity. His very intentness must have impressed her. She parted her lips as if to say something light. After looking at him—she closed them again.

Then she said, "Maybe we're going to get somewhere, after all. All right, my friend, a minute ago I wouldn't have told you anything. You've been pulled out of the twentieth century to the—well, the present. And that's all I'm going to tell you about that. I belong to a group who are opposed to the Shadows. And I was sent here after you—"

She stopped. Her brows knitted. "Never mind! Now, please, don't ask me how we knew you were here. Don't ask any more questions. This machine brought me into this room in the heart of Shadow City and it will take the two of us out if you will unjam that pin. If you don't want to go with me, loosen the pin anyway, so that I can get to"—Cargill missed the word completely —"out of here. You can stay and be murdered for all I care. Now, please, the pin!"

Murdered! That did it. It wasn't that he had forgotten. It was the insensate wriggling of his mind that pushed that danger into the background. He leaned forward, his fingers forming to take hold. "Do I pull or push?" he whispered.

"Pull."

Cargill snatched at it. The first touch startled him. It was as if he had grasped a film of oil. His skin slid over the immense smoothness of it as if there were nothing there. He grabbed again, sweating abruptly with the realization of the problem.

"Jerk!" said the girl harshly.

He jerked. And felt the slight tug as it yielded a fraction of an inch. "Got it!" It was his own voice, hoarse and triumphant.

The girl reached past him. "Quick, grab that smooth bar." Even as she spoke her hand guided his. He snatched for a hold. Her hand clutched the same bar just above where he was clinging.

He remembered then a dull glow from the bulbous section near his face. His body tingled. And then he was lying on a hard smooth floor in a large room.

3

Cargill did not look at the girl immediately. He climbed gingerly to his feet and put his hand to his head. It was an instinctive gesture, part of his absorption with himself. He found no pain, no dizziness, no sense of unbalance.

Why he had expected such reaction he didn't know. He began to brace up to the situation. With brightening eyes, he glanced around the room. It was bigger and higher than his first impression had indicated. It was made of marble and seemed to be an anteroom. Except for minor seating arrangements for temporary visitors it had virtually no furniture. There was a high arched doorway at either long end of the room, but in each case the doors merely opened onto a wide hallway. A single large window to Cargill's left faced onto shubbery, so he could not see what was beyond.

He was staring avidly at the window when he became aware that the girl was watching him with an ironic smile. Cargill turned and looked at her. "Why shouldn't I be curious?" he asked defensively.

"Go right ahead," she said. She giggled. "But you look funny."

He stared at her angrily. She was a much smaller girl than he had thought and somewhat older. He remembered her language and decided she was probably around twenty-five—and unmarried. Young married women with children watched their tongues. And besides, they didn't go out risking their lives by joining exotic groups of adventurous rebels.

The shrewdness of the analysis pleased Cargill. It helped to relax his taut mind. For the first time since leaving the cell, he thought, "Why, I'm way up in the future! And this time I'm free." He had a sudden desperate desire to see everything before he was returned to the twentieth century. A will came: to know, to experience. He had a thrill of imminent pleasure. Once more he whirled toward the window. Then again he stopped, remembering what the girl had said: "you look funny."

He glared down at his body. He was naked except for a pair of something similar to gym shorts. His clothing was not exactly indecent but Cargill felt irritated, as if he had been caught in an embarrassing position. His legs were hard and strong, but they looked thinner than they actually were. He had never been at his best in a bathing suit.

He said in annoyance, "You could have had some clothes waiting for me here. It's getting chilly."

It was. Through the window he could see that it was also becoming darker. If he were still in California then the late afternoon sea breezes were probably blowing outside. Even in midsummer that meant coolness.

The girl said casually, "One of the men will bring you something. You're to leave here as soon as it becomes dark."

"Oh!" said Cargill.

He shook his head as if he would drive out the blur that was confusing him. All these minutes he had been standing here, adjusting to the simpler aspects of his new environment. They were important—it was true— but they were the tiniest segment of all that was happening to him.

His restlessness derived from several major facts. He was in this far future world because an inter-time psychological society was using him to cure one of its patients. The morality of that was a little too deep for Cargill, but just thinking about it brought a surge of fury. What kind of curative agency was it, murdering him to soothe somebody else's upset nerves?

He fought down the anger, because danger was temporarily behind him. Ahead was the mystery of the group that had rescued him and that, tonight, intended to take him—elsewhere.

Cargill parted his lips to ask the question that quivered in his mind when the girl said, "I'll leave you here to look around. I've got to go and talk to somebody. Do not follow me, please."

She was at the door to the left of the window before Cargill could find his voice. "Just a minute," he said. "I want to ask some questions."

"I don't doubt it," said Ann Reece, with a low laugh. "You may ask *him* later." She turned and was gone before he could speak again.

Being alone soothed him. The presence of other people while he was trying to adjust had been a severe pressure upon him. Everybody else appeared to have plans about and for him. He had none for himself except perhaps to see more of what was outside the window.

Peering out through the glass, Cargill had the initial impression that he was looking onto a well-kept park. The impression changed. For through the lattice work of the shrubbery he could see a street. It was the kind of street men dream about in moments of magical imagination. It wound through tall trees, among palms and fruit trees. It had shop windows fronting oddly shaped buildings that nestled among the greenery. Hidden lights spread a mellow brightness into the curves and corners. The afternoon had become quite dark and every window glowed as from some inner warmth. He had a tantalizing vision of interiors that were different from anything he had ever seen.

All this came from only a glimpse as viewed through the lattice work of a rose arbor. Cargill drew back, trembling. He had had his first look at a city of hundreds of years in the future. It was an exhilarating experience.

He took another long look, but what he could see was too fragmentary to satisfy his expanding need. He retreated from that fascinating view and peered through the door beyond which the girl had disappeared. He saw the hallway, lit by a drab light that reflected from another doorway some score of feet to the right. He hesitated. Ann Reece had forbidden him to follow her, but she had made no threats. He was still standing there. undecided, when he grew aware that a man and woman were talking in the lighted room.

Cargill strained his ears. But he could hear nothing of what was said. It was the tone of the man's voice that interested him. He seemed to be giving instructions and the girl was protesting. Cargill recognized Ann Reece's voice. He noted how subdued it was. Her reaction dictated his own. This was not the time to barge in on her—better to sit down and wait.

He was halfway across the room, heading toward a chair, when his foot struck something that clanged metallically. In the almost complete darkness it took a moment to recognize the machine that had brought him and the girl out of the glass-walled room. Gazing at the strange object, conscious of the wonder of it, Cargill had a wild thought—if he could take this machine and sneak off into the descending night, then he'd be free not only of his original captors but also of the new group with its schemes. That last was important, now that he had heard the determined voice of the man in the next room.

Like a burglar in the night Cargill knelt beside the instrument. It was two-headed, like a barbell used by weight-lifters. In the gloom, his quick eyes searched for the "pin" that had caused the earlier trouble. It was not visible. Using only the tips of his fingers, he pushed the bar, rolling it slowly. It was warm to his touch but showed no other animation. Cargill withdrew his fingers. This was not really the time to test its power.

Uncertain, he climbed to his feet. He became aware that footsteps were coming along the hallway. He turned to face the doorway. The footsteps entered the room, there was a rustling sound and the place blazed with light.

A Shadow shape stood in the doorway.

Shadow shape, shadow substance . . . shadow. Cargill's mind kept trying to play a trick on him, kept trying to put solidity where there was nothing but form. He could see the wall through the shadowy thing; and yet, even as he saw it, he tried to blot out the reality of it.

His gaze finally stopped jumping, and he saw that he was looking at a ghost-like human shape, a gaseous, dark being, an improbable creature, a human thing that said:

"He's one of them all right. I can detect nothing."

From a point close behind Cargill, Ann Reece said, "About how many are there?"

"Not more than a dozen in this whole area of time. It's an interesting phenomenon."

The conversation was both literally and figuratively over Cargill's head. There was the statement that he was an interesting phenomenon; and to Cargill, who had been under enormous strain for many hours, that was funny—considering the fantastic phenomenon that had said it. He began to laugh, uncontrollably. He laughed until the tears came to his eyes, and then, weakening, laughed until he sank down on the floor. He was lying there, exhausted, when something touched him, and he had a sense of being—*moved*.

He was walking. It was hard to understand how it had happened, but he could feel the pressure of the dirt under his shoes and the play of muscles in his legs as they moved back and forth.

For a long time, in the reflection of the flashlight in the hands of the girl, he watched the rise and fall of her heels. Every little while she kicked up loose soil. The soft sounds suddenly shocked the blur out of Cargill's mind. His legs continued their automatic movement, but his brain flashed to awareness of his environment.

It was pitch dark. There was no sign of a city. He seemed to be on an unpaved rural road. Cargill looked up. But the sky must have been thick with clouds for he saw no stars and no moon. Cargill groaned inwardly. What could have happened? One instant he was in a large marble anteroom inside a city; then the shadow shape had come in and seemed to examine him—one look, a few words—and then, this dark road behind a silent companion.

"Ann!" said Cargill softly. "Ann Reece."

She did not turn or pause. "So you're coming out of it," she said.

Cargill wondered briefly just what it was he was coming out of. Amnesia, certainly—temporary amnesia. The thought faded. To a man who had been unconscious several times now, another period of blankness didn't matter.

Here he was. That was what counted. "Where are we going?" he asked, and his voice was quite normal.

The girl's tone oddly suggested she was shrugging. "Couldn't leave you in the city," she said.

"Why not?"

"The Shadows would get you."

The phrase had an irritating rhythm that snatched Cargill's attention. *The Shadows will get you. The Shadows will get you.* He could almost imagine children being frightened by the threat.

His thought poised on the fact that at least one Shadow had seen him. He said as much. There was a pause. "He's not . . . one of them," she finally answered.

"Who is he?"

"He has a plan"—she hesitated—"for fighting them."

Cargill's mind made a single, embracing leap. "Where do I fit into this plan?"

Silence answered. Cargill waited, then strode forward and fell in step beside her. "Tell me," he said.

"It's very complicated." She still did not turn her head. "We had to have somebody from a time far past so the Shadows couldn't use their four-dimensional minds on him. He looked at you and said he couldn't tell what your future was. Here and there through history are individuals who are . . . complicated . . . like that. You're the one we selected."

"Selected!" Cargill exclaimed. Then he was silent. He had an abrupt impossible picture that everything that had happened to him had been planned. In his mind's eye he saw a drunken soldier being selected to wreck a car and kill a girl. No, wait, that couldn't be. He had deliberately got drunk that night. They couldn't have had anything to do with that.

His tense speculation subsided. The possibilities were too intricate. With a cold intentness he stared at the indistinct profile of Ann Reece. "I want to know," he said, "what way I'm supposed to be used."

"I don't know," she said. "I'm only a pawn."

His fingers snatched at her arm. "Like heck you don't know," he said roughly. "Where are you taking me?"

The fingers of her other hand tugged futilely at his hand.

She struggled a little. "You're hurting my arm," she whimpered.

Reluctantly Cargill released her. "You can answer my question."

"I'm taking you to a hiding place of ours. You'll be told there what's next." Her tone was strained.

Cargill pondered the possibilities and liked them less every second. Things *were* moving too fast, but a few facts stood out. It seemed certain now that he was not in the twentieth century. His brief view of the shadow-shape was already becoming unbelievable, but the recollection still had enough substance to establish this entire affair as something apart from the world as he had known it. Equally convincing as data was the transportation device Ann Reece had used to bring him from the room in Shadow City.

His thoughts on how all this had come about were not quite so clear. There were conflicting stories. The Inter-Time Society for Psychological Adjustment had in a routine fashion brought him to the future to play a part in the therapeutic conditioning of one of its clients. It sounded fantastic—and it was difficult to grasp how Marie Chanette's descendant could have carried through with such an idea—but that was definitely the implication she had presented to him. That was also the reality behind the statements made by the disembodied voice in that queer double apartment. No one there seemed to have anticipated the arrival of Ann Reece.

Her appearance on the scene introduced a new set of factors that would be harder to think through. "She said it," he thought, "they chose me." That changed the picture. He was no longer just Effect. He was Cause, though in a way that was not definable as yet; he was Cause in that he had something which some-body wanted.

The group behind Ann Reece intended to use him against beings they feared, which again implied that he had something which made him useful. What was it she had said? His future could not be predicted. Well, whose future could? If they meant that having pulled him away from his own time, they could no longer keep track of his actions—well, that seemed rather natural. However, she had made a precise statement: *Here and there through history are individuals who are complicated.* What made him complicated?

He had been walking along, frowning, as he tried to think logically over what had happened. Finally, he said, "I really don't like this situation at all. I feel as if I shouldn't go with you to this hiding place."

That didn't seem to worry her. "Don't be silly," she said. "Where would you go?"

Cargill pondered that uneasily. Once, in Korea, his unit had withdrawn in disorder, and had been in enemy territory for two days. He could imagine that a similar predicament here might be equally unhappy. Undecided, he looked down at himself. He was aware that he wore clothes. However, in the night dimness, it was impos-sible to see what they were like. But he did feel warm and cozy. Surely, conspicuous clothing wouldn't have been given him. Abruptly, he made up his mind.

"I don't think," he said quietly, "that I'm going any farther in your direction. Good-by."

He stepped away from her and ran rapidly along the road, heading the way they had come. After not more than ten seconds he plunged off the road and found himself scrambling through thick brush. Ann Reece's flashlight flared behind him, obviously seeking him. But the reflections from the beam only made it easier for him to penetrate the brush.

He broke into a meadow and trotted across it—and then he was in brush again. For the first time he heard her voice calling. "You fool, you! Come back!" For several minutes, her words broke the spell of the night but he heard only snatches now. Once he thought she said, "Watch out for the Planiacs!" But that didn't make sense. He passed over the crest of a hill and thereafter heard her no more.

Purposefully, though carefully, Cargill pressed on through the darkness. He grew startled at the extent of the wilderness, but it was important that he keep moving. In the morning a search might be made for him, and he had better be as far as possible from the road where he had left Ann Reece. The night was dark, the sky continued sullen. The tangy smell of water warned him that he was approaching either a river or a lake. Cargill turned aside. He was crossing what seemed to be an open space when, out of the night, the beam of a flashlight focused on him.

A girl's high-pitched voice said, "Darn you, I've got my spitter on you." It sounded like "spitter." "Put up your hands."

In the reflections of the flashlight, Cargill glimpsed a dull metal gadget that looked like nothing else than an elongated radio tube. It pointed at him steadily.

The girl raised her voice in a yell. "Hey, Pa, I've caught myself a Tweener." The word sounded like

"Tweener." The girl went on excitedly, "Come on, Pa, and help me get him aboard."

Afterward, Cargill realized this was the moment he should have tried to escape. It was the unnatural weapon that held him indecisive. Had it been an ordinary gun he'd have dived off into the darkness—or so he told himself when it was too late.

Before he could decide, a roughly dressed man loped out of the darkness. "Good work, Lela," he said. "You're a smart girl."

Cargill had a quick glimpse of a lean, rapacious, bearded countenance. And then the man had taken up a position behind him and was jabbing another of the tubelike weapons into him.

"Get going, stranger, or I'll spit you."

Cargill started forward reluctantly. Ahead of him a long, snub-nosed, snub-tailed structure loomed vaguely out of the darkness. The light from the flash reflected from the object's glassy surface. And then—

"Follow Lela through that door."

Now there was no escape. The man and the weapon crowded behind him. Cargill found himself in a large, dimly lighted room, amazingly well constructed and looking both cozy and costly. Urged across the carpeted floor, he moved through a comfortable lounge into a narrow corridor and toward a tiny room that was even more dimly lighted than the first one.

A few moments later, while the man glowered in the doorway, the girl fastened a chain around Cargill's right and left ankles. A key clicked twice; then she was drawing back, saying, "There's a cot in that corner."

His two captors retreated along the corridor toward the brighter light, the girl babbling happily about having "caught one of them at last."

The man said, "Maybe we'd better cast adrift. Maybe there's more of them."

The light in Cargill's room went out. There was a jerk and then a slow upward movement. Cargill thought, amazed, *an airship!*

His mind jumped back to what Ann Reece had shouted at him: "Watch out for the Planiacs!" Had she meant—this? Carefully, in the darkness he edged towards the cot the girl had indicated. He reached it and sank down wearily.

He spent about a minute fumbling over the chain with his fingers. The metal was hard, the chain itself just over a foot long, an excellent length for hobbling a man.

He was suddenly too tired to think further. He lay down and fell asleep immediately.

4

Cargill had a lazy sensation of drifting along. For some reason he resisted waking up, and kept sinking back into the darkness. Throughout that early dreamy stage he had no memory of what had happened or of where he was. Gradually, however, he grew conscious of motion underneath him. He stirred and felt the chain clasps against his ankles. That jarred him and brought the beginning of alarm. With a start he woke up.

His eyes took in the curving metal ceiling, and all too swiftly he remembered. He reached down and touched the chain. It was cool and hard and convincing to his touch, and gave him an empty feeling. And then, just as he was about to sit up, he realized he was not alone. He started to turn his head. He caught a glimpse of what was there barely in time to bring his hands up in front of his face.

A whip cracked across his fingers and licked at his neck, stinging and burning the skin. "Get up, you lazy good-for-nothing." The man who stood in the doorway was already drawing the whip for another blow.

With a gasp Cargill swung his legs from the cot to the

floor. In a black rage he was about to launch himself at the figure when the metallic rattle of the chain reminded him that he was desperately handicapped. That dimmed his fury and brought a sense of disaster.

Once more the whip struck at him. Cargill ducked and managed to get part of the blow on the sleeve of his coat. The thin sharp end flicked harmlessly past his shoulder against the metal wall.

Again the whip was drawn back.

He had already recognized his assailant as the companion of the girl the night before. Seen in the light of day he was a scrawny slovenly individual about forty years old. Several days' growth of beard darkened his face. His lips were thin. His eyes had a curiously crafty expression, and his face was a mask of bad temper. He wore a pair of greasy trousers and his filthy shirt, which was open at the neck, revealed a flat hairy chest. He stood with an animal-like snarl on his face. "Darn your hide, get going."

Cargill thought: "If he tries to hit me again, I'll rush him."

Aloud he temporized. "What do you want me to do?"

That seemed to add new fury to the man's anger. "I'll learn you what I want!"

The whip came up and it would have flashed down except for Cargill's lunge from the cot. The violent impact of their coming together nearly took his breath away but it smashed his assailant against the metal door jamb.

The man released a screech and tried to pull back. But Cargill had him now. With one hand he clutched the fellow's shirt and with the other he clenched and struck at the narrow bony jaw.

It was a knockout. A limp body collapsed to the floor. Cargill followed, kneeling awkwardly, and with trembling fingers started to search the other's pockets.

From farther along the corridor, the girl's voice said, "All right, put up your hands or I'll spit you."

Cargill jerked up, tensed for action. He hesitated as he saw the weapon, then reluctantly drew back from the man's body. Stiffly, he sat down on the cot.

The girl walked forward and dug the toe of her shoe into her father's ribs. "Get up, you fool," she said.

The man stirred and sat up. "I'll kill him," he mumbled. "I'll murder that blasted Tweener." It still sounded like "Tweener."

The girl was contemptuous. "You aren't going to kill anybody. You asked for a kick in the teeth and you got it. What did you want him to do?"

The man stood up groggily and felt his jaw. "These darn Tweeners," he said, "make me sick with their sleeping in, and not knowing what to do."

The girl said coldly, "Don't be such a fool, Pa. He hasn't been trained yet. Do you expect him to read your mind?" She squeezed past him and came into the little room. "And besides, you keep your dirty hands off him. I caught him, and I'll do any beating that's necessary. Give me that whip."

"Look, Lela Bouvy," said her father, "I'm the boss of this floater and don't you forget it." But he handed her the whip and said sullenly, "All I want is some breakfast and I want it quick."

"You'll get it. Now beat it." She motioned imperiously. "I'll do the rest."

The man turned and slouched out of sight.

The girl gestured with her thumb. "All right, you, into the kitchen."

Cargill hesitated, half-minded to resist. But the word, kitchen, conjured thoughts of food. He realized he was tremendously hungry. Silently he climbed to his feet and hobbled clumsily through the door she indicated. He was thinking, "These creatures could keep me chained up here from now on."

The despair that came was like a weight, more constricting than the chain that bound him.

The kitchen proved to be a narrow corridor between thick translucent walls. It was about ten feet long and at the far end was a closed transparent door, beyond which he could see machinery. Both the kitchen and the machine room were bright with the light that flooded through the translucent walls. Cargill glanced around, puzzled. There was no sign of a stove or of any standard cooking equipment. He saw no food, no dishes, no cupboards. Looking for lines in the glass-like walls, he saw hundreds that were horizontal, vertical, diagonal, curving and circular. They seemed to have no purpose. If any of them marked off a panel or a door he couldn't see it.

He turned questioningly to the girl. She spoke first. "No clouds this morning. We'll be able to get all the heat we want."

He watched, interested, as she reached up with one hand, spread it wide and touched the top of the wall where it curved toward the ceiling. Only her thumb and little finger actually touched the glass. With a quick movement she lightly ran her hand parallel to the floor. A thick slab of the glass broke free along an intricate series of lines and noiselessly slid down into a slot. Cargill craned his neck. From where he stood he could just see that there was a limpidly transparent panel inside, behind which were shelves. What was on the shelves, he could not see.

Casually, the girl slid the panel sideways. For a moment her body hid what she was doing. When she drew back, she held a plate on which were raw fish and potatoes. It looked like trout, and surprisingly it had been cleaned. Yet neither Bouvy nor his daughter looked as if they would do anything in advance of need.

He shrewdly suspected the presence of kitchen gadgets that could automatically scale and fillet a fish.

The girl took a few steps toward him. Once more she ran her little finger and thumb along the upper wall. Another section of the sunlit wall slid down and there was a second panel with shelves behind it. Opening the panel, she placed the plate on one of the shelves.

As she closed the panel a faint steam rose from the fish, turning it a golden brown. The potatoes lost their hard whiteness and visibly underwent the chemical change to a cooked state.

"That'll do, I guess," said Lela Bouvy. She added, "You better get yourself a bite."

She took out the plate with her bare hands, paused at the refrigerator to take out an apple and a pear from a bottom shelf and walked out, still carrying the plate.

Cargill was left alone in the kitchen. By the time she returned for her own breakfast, he had eaten an apple, cooked himself some chicken legs and potatoes and was busily eating when she paused in the doorway.

She was rather a pretty thing if one allowed for a certain sullenness of expression. So it seemed to Cargill. Her hair was not too well combed but it was not tangled, and it had a pleasant shine that indicated she lavished some attention on it. Her eyes were a hot blue, her lips full, and her chin came to a point. She wore dungarees and an open-necked shirt which partly exposed a very firm tanned bust.

She said, with a suspicious tone in her voice, "How did a smart-looking Tweener like you come to get caught so easy?"

Cargill swallowed a large mouthful of potato in several quick gulps and said, "I'm not a Tweener."

The hot blue of her eyes smoldered with easy anger. "What kind of a smarty answer is that?"

Cargill cleaned up what was left on the plate and said, "I'm being honest with you. I'm not a Tweener."

She frowned. "Then what are you?" She stiffened, the anger leaving her eyes, making them appear to change color. She whispered, "Not a Shadow?"

Before he could pretend or even decide not to, she answered her own question. "Of course you aren't. A Shadow would know all about this ship and how the kitchen works without having to watch me first. They fix our ships for us floater folk when the repair job is too hard for us to figure out."

The moment for pretense, whatever its possibilities might have been, was past. Cargill said grudgingly, "No, I'm not a Shadow."

The girl's frown had deepened. "But a Tweener would've known that too." She looked at him warily. "What's your name?"

"Morton Cargill."

"Where are you from?"

Cargill told her and watched those expressive eyes of hers change color again. Finally she nodded. "One of those, eh?" She seemed disturbed. "We get a reward for people like you."

She broke off. "What did you do—back where you came from—to start the Shadows after you?"

Cargill shrugged. "Nothing." He had no intention of launching into a detailed account of the Marie Chanette incident.

Once more the blue eyes were flashing. "Don't you dare lie to me," she said. "All I've got to do is to tell Pa that you're a getaway and that'll cook your goose."

Cargill said with all the earnestness he could muster,

"I can't help that. I really don't know." He hesitated, then said, "What year is this?"

The moment he had asked the question he felt breathless.

5

He hadn't thought about it before. He hadn't had time. The clock in the glass-walled room in Shadow City had indicated that it was May 6th but not the year. Everything had happened too swiftly. Even his hazy questions to Ann Reece during those first minutes after arrival had been so weighted with emotion that the possibilities of being actually in the future hadn't fully penetrated.

Which future? What year? What had happened during the centuries that must have passed? Where? How? Who? He caught his whirling mind, fastened it down, brought it to focus. The most important fact was—what year?

Lela Bouvy shrugged and said, "Two Thousand Three Hundred and Ninety-One."

Cargill ventured, "What I can't understand is how the world has changed so completely from my time." He described the United States of 1954.

The girl was calm. "It was natural. Most people want to be free, not to have to live in one place or to be tied to some stupid work. The world isn't completely free yet. We floater folk are the only lucky ones so far."

Cargill had his own idea of a freedom where individuals depended on somebody else to repair their machines. But he was interested in information, not in exploding false notions. He said cautiously, "How many floater folk are there?"

"About fifteen million."

She spoke glibly but Cargill let the figure pass.

"And the Tweeners?" he asked.

"Three million or so." She was contemptuous. "The cowards live in cities."

"What about the Shadows?"

"A hundred thousand, maybe a little more or less. Not much."

Cargill guessed that she could not possibly know that those figures were accurate. She didn't appear the type of person who would be well-informed on such matters. But she did provide a picture of the age, and it filled a gap in his knowledge. He visualized wilderness, a few cities, vast numbers of floaters prowling at random through the lower skies. He nodded half to himself, parted his lips, and began: "I gather that the Shadows rule the roost."

"Nobody rules nobody," said Lela irritably. "And now, you've asked just about enough questions. You can mind your own business."

She went out.

Cargill was left alone most of the rest of the day. He saw Lela briefly again when she came in and prepared lunch for herself and her father.

It was not till afternoon that he started to think seriously about what he had learned. The population collapse depressed him. It made the big fight of life seem suddenly less important. All the eager ambition of the twentieth century was now proved valueless, destroyed by a catastrophe that derived not from physical force, but apparently from a will to escape. Perhaps the pressures of civilization had been too great. People had fled from it as from a plague the moment a real opportunity arose.

However, even in retrospect such a likelihood seemed improbable. Civilization had seemed so firmly intrenched. Scientifically, culturally, man had attained a high point indeed. Although his activities as a social animal left much to be desired, he was perpetually striving, seeking, learning. . . . Somewhere there must have been an intolerable rigidity, a basic falseness. By implication, from what the girl had said, Cargill guessed the answer: Authority had once more attained too great a position. In response, people had flung themselves away from a civilization that, more and more, told them that they knew nothing, that they must conform to patterns laid down for them by those who knew, or rather by those who had the legal right to know.

Instinctively, they had tried to return to a state of being Cause instead of Effect. They had rejected the hierarchy of intellect which, ever frigid, never dynamic, sought always to impose restrictions. Men had fought up from a thousand dark ages, each time to meet the same blind control forces, each time to surrender for a while to a growing mass of chains; and then—taking alarm—struggling as blindly to escape.

It seemed pretty disheartening to realize that it had happened again, to realize that the supersalesmen and the advertising executives, and the TV geniuses, and the Cadillacs and the Buicks and the Jaguars had not been able to maintain their glamor-hold. . . . Something had certainly been missing. Maybe it was the right to self-determination.

The kitchen had grown dark when Cargill became aware of the ship sinking to a lower level. He didn't realize just how low until he heard the metal shell under him whisk against the upper branches of trees. A minute later there was a thud and then a shock. The floater dragged for several feet along the ground and came to a stop. Cargill grew conscious of a muffled roaring sound outside.

Lela came into the room. Or rather, she walked straight through to the kitchen. Cargill had a sudden suspicion of what she planned to do and lurched to his feet. He was too late. The door of the engine room was open, and the girl was in the act of lowering a section of the glass wall. As he watched she eased down a hinged section of the outer wall and stepped through, out of sight. A damp sea breeze blew into Cargill's face and now he heard the roar of the surf.

The girl came back after about a minute and paused in his room. "You can go outside if you want," she said. She hesitated. Then, "Don't try to run away. You won't get far, and Pa might burn you with a spit gun."

Cargill said ruefully, "Where would I run to? I guess you folks are stuck with me."

He watched her narrowly to see how she took that. She seemed relieved. It was not a positive reaction but it was suggestive and fitted with his feeling that Lela Bouvy would welcome the presence of someone other than her father. As he hobbled through the kitchen a moment later, Cargill silently justified the plan he had of winning the girl's confidence. A prisoner in his situation was entitled to use every trick and device necessary to his escape.

He did not pause at the engine room door—how it opened, he would discover in the morning. He manipulated his chained legs down a set of steps—part of the outer wall, folded out and down on hinges. A moment later he stepped onto a sandy beach.

They spent most of the evening catching crabs and other sea creatures that crowded around a light which

Bouvy lowered into the water. It was a wild seacoast, rocky except for brief stretches of sand. In places, a primeval forest came down almost to the edge of the rock that overlooked the restless sea below. Lela scooped up the tiny creatures with a little net and tossed them onto a pile where Cargill with his fingers separated the wanted from the unwanted. It was easy to pick out and throw back the ones that Lela pointed out as inedible, to toss the others into a pail. Periodically, the girl took a pailful of the delicacies back to the floater.

She was in a visible state of exhilaration. Her eyes flashed with excitement in the light reflections, her face was alive with color. Her lips parted, her nostrils dilated. Several times when Bouvy had moved farther from hearing she shrieked at Cargill, "Isn't it fun? Isn't this the life?"

"Wonderful!" Cargill yelled back. Once he added, "I've never seen anything like it."

That seemed to satisfy her and to a point it was true. There was a pleasure to open-air living. What she didn't seem to understand was that there was more to being alive than living outdoors. Civilized life had many facets, not just one.

What concerned Cargill was the possibility that he might actually have to get used to this kind of existence. Indeed, it might be wise if he did. Here, in these free spaces, he might easily lose himself for a lifetime. Just what that would mean in terms of boredom, a sense of futility, he was not quite prepared to consider. At the moment, the prospect of such a limited life had frightening aspects.

It was well after midnight before their activities ceased, and he was back in his cot, considering the events of the night. It struck him finally that the girl's actions had been most significant. Her seeking him out frequently, her attempt to convince him of the pleasures of floater life—they added up in very meaningful fashion; and he had had just enough experience with women to guess that she was lonely. Whether her goal included lovemaking, or rather, on what terms it would include love, depended on her upbringing. He surmised prudishness from the way she held herself. However, at the moment, he felt unprepared to take the preliminary actions necessary to overcome the resistance of the simple-minded girl.

She came into his part of the ship a dozen times the next day. Cargill, who had unsuccessfully sought the secret of how to open the engine-room door, finally asked her how it was done. She showed him without hesitation. It was a matter of simultaneously touching both door jambs.

When she had gone Cargill headed directly for the engine room, paused for a moment to study the engine —that proved a futile task, since it was completely closed in—and then slid the wall section into the floor and looked down at the ground beneath.

The world that sped by below was a wilderness, but of a curious sort. As far as the eye could see were the trees and shrubery associated with land, almost untouched by the hand and metal of man. But standing amid weeds and forests were buildings. Even from a third of a mile up those that Cargill saw looked uninhabited. Brick chimneys lay tumbled over on faded roofs. Windows seen from a distance yawned emptily, or gazed up at him with a glassy stare. Barns sagged unevenly, and here and there the wood, or brick, or stone had completely collapsed, and the unpainted ruin drooped wearily to the ground.

In the beginning the only structures he saw were farmhouses and their outbuildings. But abruptly a town flowed by underneath. Now the effect of uninhabited desolation was clearly marked—tottering fences, cracked pavement overgrown by weeds, and the same design of disintegration in the houses. When they had passed over a second long-abandoned town Cargill closed the panel that had concealed the window and returned uneasily to his cot.

Coming as he did from a world in which virtually every acre of tillable land was owned and used by somebody, he was shocked by the way vast areas had been allowed to revert to a primitive state. He tried to visualize from what the girl had told him and from what he had observed how the devastation might have happened. But that got him nowhere. He wondered if the development of machinery had finally made agriculture unnecessary. If it had, then this stretch of decay and disrepair were but signs of transition. The time would come when these ghost farms and ghost towns and perhaps ghost cities would return to the soil from which they had, in their complex fashion, sprung. The time would come when these costly monuments of an earlier civilization would be as gone and forgotten as the cities of antique times.

Two more evenings were spent fishing. On the fourth day Cargill heard a woman's loud voice talking from the living room. It was an unpleasant voice and it startled him.

Curiously, he hadn't previously thought of these people as being in communication with anyone else. But the woman was unmistakably giving instructions to the Bouvy father and daughter. Almost as soon as she had stopped talking Cargill felt the ship change its course. Toward dark Lela came in.

"We'll be camping with other people tonight," she said. "So you watch yourself." She sounded fretful and she went out without waiting for him to reply.

Cargill considered the possibilities with narrowed

eyes. After four days of being in hobble chains, with no sign that they would ever come off, he was ready for a change. "All I've got to do," he told himself, "is catch two people off guard." And he wouldn't have to be gentle about it either. "Careful," he thought. "Better not build my hopes too high."

Nevertheless, it seemed to him that the presence of other people might actually produce an opportunity for escape.

6

Through the open doorway Cargill caught a glimpse of the outside activity. Men walked by carrying fishing rods. The current of air that surged through brought the tangy odor of river and the damp pleasant smell of innumerable growing things.

It grew darker rapidly. Finally, Cargill could stand his confinement no longer. He stood up and, taking care not to trip over his chain, went outside and sank down on the grass. The scene that spread before him had an idyllic quality. Here and there under the trees ships were parked. There were at least a dozen that he could see, and it seemed to him that the lights of still others showed through the thick foliage along the shore. The sound of voices floated on the air and somehow they no longer sounded harsh or crude.

There was a movement in the darkness near him. Lela Bouvy settled down on the grass beside him. She said breathlessly, "Kind of fun living like this, isn't it?"

Cargill hesitated and then, somewhat to his surprise,

found himself inwardly agreeing. "There's a desire in all of us," he thought, "to return to nature." The will to relax, the impulse to lie on green grass, to listen to the rustling of leaves in an almost impalpable breeze—all that he could feel in himself. He also had the same basic urge that had driven these Planiacs to abandon the ordered slavery of civilization. He found himself saddened by the realization that the abandonment included a return to ignorance. He said aloud, "Yes, it's pretty nice."

A tall powerful-looking woman strode out of the darkness. "Where's Bouvy?" she said. A flashlight in her hand winked on and glared at Lela and Cargill. Its bright stare held steady for seconds longer than was necessary. "Well, I'll be double darned," the woman's voice said from the intense blackness behind the light, "little Lela's gone and found herself a man."

Lela snapped, "Don't be a bigger fool than you have to be, Carmean."

The woman laughed uproariously. "I heard you had a man," she said finally, "and now that I get a look at him I can see you've done yourself proud."

Lela said indifferently, "He doesn't mean a thing to me."

"Yeah?" said Carmean derisively. Abruptly she seemed to lose interest. The beam of her flashlight swept on and left them in darkness. The light focused on Pa Bouvy sitting in a chair against the side of the ship. "Oh, there you are," said the woman.

"Yup!"

The big woman walked over. "Get up and give me that chair," she said. "Haven't you got no manners?"

"Watch your tongue, you old buzzard," said Bouvy pleasantly. But he stood up and disappeared into the ship. He emerged presently with another chair.

During his absence the woman had picked up the chair in which he had been sitting and carried it some twenty-five feet down the river's bank.

She yelled at Bouvy, "Bring that contraption over here! I want to talk to you privately. Besides, I guess maybe those two love-birds want to be alone." She guffawed.

Lela said in a strained voice to Cargill, "That's Carmean. She's one of the bosses. She thinks she's being funny when she talks like that."

Cargill said, "What do you mean, one of the bosses?"

The girl sounded surprised. "She tells us what to do." She added hastily, "Of course, she can't interfere in our private life."

Cargill digested that for a moment. During the silence he could hear Carmean's voice at intervals. Only an occasional word reached him. Several times she said, "Tweeners" and "Shadows." Once she said, "It's a cinch."

There was an urgency in her voice that made him want to hear what she was saying, but presently he realized the impossibility of making sense out of stray words. He relaxed and said, "I thought you folks lived a free life—without anybody to tell you what to do and where to get off."

"You got to have rules," said Lela. "You got to know where to draw the line. What you can do and what you can't do." She added earnestly, "But we are free. Not like those Tweeners in their cities." The last was spoken scornfully.

Cargill said, "What happens if you don't do what she says?"

"You lose the benefits."

"Benefits?"

"The preachers won't preach to you," said Lela.

"Nobody gives you food. The Shadows won't fix your ship." She added casually, "And things like that."

Cargill decided he wouldn't worry about the preachers. He had once had a conversation with an army chaplain before leaving the U.S. for the Far East. The man had attempted a very colloquial approach, referring to the possibility of "going West." Cargill recalled his own analogy that Stateside "West" ended at the Pacific Ocean, and that if he could still feel his feet wet after crossing that boundary, he would begin to believe that he'd better find out how warm the water could get.

He considered most of the religious people he knew hypocrites. The implications of believing that one *was* a soul, or had one, were so numerous that anything short of acting on these implications made belief a mere protective coloring. Cargill knew of no one who showed by his actions that he believed himself to be an infinitely tenuous energy structure united to a material body.

Lela's reference to not receiving food if they didn't conform puzzled him. He had had the impression that the Planiacs garnered their living from the streams and the seashore and the wilderness. They might not be provided a bountiful living the year round, but the marvellous refrigeration and cooking systems on the floaters made large accumulations possible at the harvest seasons. And that emphasized the one important restriction in what she had said. If the Shadows wouldn't fix the ships, that indeed could be disastrous. One might conclude that the solution was to learn to fix one's own ship. It was interesting that a large number of people would let themselves be so easily controlled. It indicated that it wasn't the material side that mattered, but the belief and attitudes of a group. These people, like so many before them, were the slaves of their own thoughts.

Cargill said at long last: "Why do the Shadows recognize the authority of Carmean and the other bosses?"

"Oh, they just want us to behave."

"But you can capture Tweeners?"

The girl hesitated. Then, "Nobody seems to worry about a Tweener," she said.

Cargill nodded. He recalled his attempts to get information from her during the past few days. Apparently she hadn't then thought of these restraining influences on her life. Now, though she seemed unaware of it, she had given him a picture of a rigid social structure. Surely, he thought desperately, he could figure out some way to take advantage of this situation. He moved irritably and the chain rattled, reminding him that all the plans in the world could not directly affect metal.

Carmean, closely followed by Bouvy, brought her chair back to the ship. Setting the chair down, she walked slowly over and stood in front of Cargill. She half-turned and said, "I could use a husky guy around, Bouvy."

"He isn't for sale." That was Lela, her voice curt.

"I'm speaking to your Pa, kid, so watch your tongue."

"You heard the girl," said Bouvy. "We've got a good man here." His tone was cunning, rather than earnest. He sounded as if he were prepared to haggle but wanted the best of the deal.

Carmean said, "Don't you go getting commercial on me." She added darkly, "You'd better watch out. These Tweeners haven't got any religion when it comes to a good-looking girl."

Bouvy grunted but when he spoke he still sounded good-humored. "Don't give me any of that. Lela's going to stick with her Pa and be a help to him all her life. Aren't you, honey?"

"You talk like a fool, Pa. Better keep your mouth shut."

"She's fighting hard," said Carmean slyly. "You can see what's in the back of her mind."

Bouvy sat down in one of the chairs. "Just for the sake of the talk, Carmean," he said, "what'll you give for him?"

Cargill had listened to the early stages of the transaction with a shocked sense of unreality. But swiftly now he realized that he was in process of being sold.

It emphasized, if emphasis was needed, that to these Planiacs he was a piece of property, a chattel, a slave who could be forced to menial labor, or whipped, or even killed without anyone being concerned. His fate was a private affair which would trouble no one but himself. "Somebody's going to get gypped," he told himself angrily. A man as determined as he was to escape would be a bad bargain for Carmean or anyone else. In the final issue, he thought, he'd take all necessary risks and he had just enough front-line army experience to make that mean something.

The bargaining was still going on. Carmean offered her own ship in return for Cargill and the Bouvy ship. "It's a newer model," she urged. "It's good for ten years without any trouble or fussing."

Bouvy's hesitation was noticeable. "That isn't a fair offer," he said plaintively. "The Shadows will give you all the new ships you want. So you aren't offering me anything that means anything to you."

Carmean retorted, "I'm offering you what I can get and you can't."

"It's too much trouble," said Bouvy. "I'd have to move all our stuff."

"Your stuff!" The big woman was contemptuous. "Why, that junk isn't worth carting out! And besides, I've got a ship full of valuables over there."

Bouvy was quick. "It's a deal if you change ship for ship with everything left aboard."

Carmean laughed curtly. "You must take me for a bigger fool than I look. I'll leave you more stuff than you've ever seen but I'm taking plenty out."

Lela, who had been sitting silently, said, "You two are just talking. It makes no difference what you decide. I caught him and he's mine. That's the law, and you just try to use your position as boss to change it, Carmean."

Even in the darkness, Carmean's hesitation was apparent. Finally she said, "We'll talk about this some more tomorrow morning. Meantime, Bouvy, you'd better teach this kid of yours some manners."

"I'll do just that," said Pa Bouvy and there was a vicious undertone in his voice. "Don't you worry, Carmean. You've bought yourself a Tweener and if we have any trouble in the morning there's going to be a public whipping here of an ungrateful daughter."

Carmean laughed in triumph. "That's the kind of talk I like to hear," she said. "The old man's standing up for himself at last."

Still laughing, she walked off into the darkness. Pa Bouvy stood up.

"Lela!"

"What?"

"Get that Tweener inside the ship and chain him up good."

"Okay, Pa." She climbed to her feet. "Get a move on," she said to Cargill.

Without a word, moving slowly because of the chain, Cargill went inside and lay down on his cot.

It must have been several hours later when he awoke, aware that somebody was tugging at the chain.

"Careful," whispered Lela Bouvy, "I'm trying to unlock this. Hold still."

Cargill, tense, did as he was told. A minute later he

was free. The girl's whisper came again, "You go ahead —through the kitchen. I'll be right behind you. Careful."

Cargill was careful.

7

Cargill lay in the dark on the grass feeling no particular urge to move. The sense of being free had not yet taken firm root inside him. The night had become distinctly cooler and most of the machines were dark. Only one ship still shed light from a half-open doorway and that was more than a hundred feet along the river bank from where he crouched.

Cargill considered his first move. More quickly now he began to realize his new situation. He need only creep out of this camp and then go where he pleased. At least it seemed for a moment as if that was all he had to do. However, he felt reluctant to take the first move.

In the darkness, progress would be difficult and morning might find him still dangerously close to the Planiacs. He imagined himself being seen from the air. He pictured a search party with an air support, finding him within a few hours after dawn. The possibilities chilled him and brought the first change in his purpose. "If I could steal one of these ships," he thought indecisively.

There was a faint sound beside him and then the whispered voice of Lela Bouvy said, "I want you to take her ship. That's the only way I'll let you go."

Cargill turned in the darkness. Her words implied that she had a weapon to force him to obey her. But the darkness under the trees was too intense for him to see if she were armed. He didn't have to be told that "her ship" referred to Carmean's. His response must have been too slow. Once more Lela spoke.

"Get going."

Carmean's ship was as good as any, Cargill decided. He whispered, "Which is hers?"

"The one that's got a light."

"Oh!"

Some of his gathering determination faded. Carmean asleep and Carmean awake were two different propositions. In spite of his qualms he began to move forward. He could at least investigate the situation before making up his mind. A few minutes later he paused behind a tree about a dozen feet from Carmean's ship. The dim light that streamed from the partly open doorway made a vague patch of brightness on the grass. Near the edge of that dully lighted area Carmean herself sat on the grass.

Cargill, who had been about to start forward again, saw her just in time. He stopped with a gulp and it was only slowly that the tension of that narrow escape left him. He glanced back finally and saw Lela in the act of moving toward him. Hastily Cargill headed her off. He drew her into the shelter of a leafy plant, explained the situation, and asked, "Is there anybody else in the ship?"

"No. Her last husband fell off the ship three months ago. At least that was what Carmean said happened. She's been looking for another one ever since, but none of the men'll have her. That's why she wanted you."

It was a new idea to Cargill. He had a momentary mental picture of himself in the role of a chained husband. It shocked him. The sooner he got away from these people, the better off he'd be. And in view of their casually ruthless plans for him he need feel no sense of restraint. He whispered to Lela, "I'll jump on her and bang her over the head. Have you got anything I can hit her with?" He felt savage and merciless. He hoped the girl would give him her gun. Just for an instant then, as she slipped something metallic into his hand, he thought she had done so.

She whispered fiercely, "That's from the edge of your cot. It'll look as if you got free and took it along as a weapon."

Her logic was not entirely convincing to Cargill, but he saw that she was trying to convince herself. And it was important that there be some kind of explanation for his escape. Bouvy would undoubtedly be furious with her.

Cautiously, Cargill stole forward. As he reached the shelter of the tree near Carmean the big woman climbed heavily to her feet.

"So you finally got her, Grannis," she said to somebody Cargill couldn't see.

"Yes," said a voice from the other side of the tree behind which Cargill, rigid now, crouched. The man's voice went on, "I couldn't make it any sooner."

"So long as you could make it at all," said Carmean indifferently. "Let's go inside."

Just what he expected then, Cargill had no idea. He had a brief, bitter conviction that he ought to attack boh the stranger and Carmean and then:

A Shadow walked into the lighted area.

Morton Cargill stayed where he was, behind the tree. His first feeling of intense disappointment yielded to the realization that there was still hope. This was a secret midnight meeting. The Shadow who had come to talk to Carmean would leave presently, and there'd be another opportunity to seize the ship.

He began cautiously to back away and then he stopped. It seemed to him suddenly that perhaps he ought to overhear what was being said. He was planning how he could do it when Lela slipped up behind him.

"What's the matter?" she whispered angrily. "Why are you standing there?"

"Sh-h-hh!" said Cargill. That was almost automatic. He was intent on his own purposes, feeling now that anything that concerned the Shadows could concern him. "I've got to remember," he told himself, "that I was brought here by someone who intended to use me."

His capture by Lela was an unfortunate incident not on the schedule of the original planners. He paid no attention to the girl but slipped from behind the tree and headed for Carmean's floater. He reached the door safely and flattened himself against the metal wall beside it.

Almost immediately, he had his first disappointment. The voices inside were too far away from him to hear. As had happened when Carmean talked to Pa Bouvy earlier, only occasional words came through.

Once, a man's voice said: "When was that? I don't recall agreeing to that."

A little later, Carmean's voice lifted to audible pitch on a triumphant note. "Don't worry about us. We'll be ready in case there's a hitch-up."

The voices came closer.

"All right now," the Shadow was saying, "let's go and get this man Cargill. I won't feel right until he's safely in our hands again."

Cargill waited for no more. Swiftly, but cautiously,

he backed away along the side of the ship. In the darkness under the curving nose of the machine he crouched tensely. The light on the grass in front of the door brightened as the door was opened wider. The Shadow stepped out.

Beyond and through him, a tree was visible. He had a head and body shaped like a man, and as he paused, half turning, waiting for Carmean, his eyes were clearly visible. They were shadow eyes for they did not glitter in the light. But dull though they were, they were unmistakably eyes.

Carmean came out. She said, "I want to get this straight. I keep this guy Cargill in my ship until I hear from you?" There was satisfaction in her tone.

"Exactly," was the grim reply. "And if I send word bring him without delay. You'll get all the men you want when the time comes." He broke off. "Which ship?"

Cargill didn't catch what Carmean said but she must have indicated the direction. They moved off, out of the spread of light into the greater darkness.

Lela came hurrying from her hiding place. She paused breathless in the night beside him. "Quick," she whispered. "We'll have to get aboard and leave."

"We?" said Cargill. There was no time to talk about the implication of the plural. Clear and loud in the night air came the sound of a knock on metal and then Carmean's voice.

"Bouvy, open up! It's me."

The discovery of his escape was seconds away. Cargill reached the doorway of Carmean's ship, paused only long enough to let Lela get in ahead of him and then he was inside.

"You get the ship into the air," he whispered. "I'll hold them off here." He wasn't sure just what he would do against guns but he had a vague notion that it was important to keep the door open until the ship was actually rising into the air.

There was a prolonged pause and then: the ship tugged slightly under him. Cargill held his breath, counting the seconds as the floater drifted upward.

Presently, with shaking fingers, he closed the door and called to Lela, "Can you turn off the lights?"

There was silence, then darkness. Cautiously Cargill opened the door again and carefully he peered out. The top of a tree glided by, only inches below. The slow way in which it passed from sight emphasized that the speed of these light-powered ships at night was negligible.

Lela's voice came faintly from forward. "I'm trying to get her out over the river. There'll be more light there. Anybody following?"

Cargill couldn't be sure. He was looking down slantingly at a camp that was slowly coming to life. Even that minimum activity was fairly well hidden behind dense foliage. He saw splashes of light and there was the sound of excited voices. But if any ship rose up to follow them during those first minutes Cargill did not see it.

Under him the machine seemed to quicken its pace. He looked down and saw that they were over the river. And now he could understand Lela's purpose. The water was alive with light reflections. He estimated that they were traveling at least ten miles an hour.

The camp slowly vanished behind a bend in the river. When he could no longer see it, he closed the door and headed for the all-room. It was somewhat larger than the similar room in the Bouvys' ship but it was functionally the same. He glanced into the control room.

Lela was in the control chair. She did not look at him. Cargill hesitated, then went back to the door. He opened it and spent the next hour gazing into the night. The moon came up while he sat there and the ship accelerated perceptibly. They were still only a few feet above the forest.

8

The minister listened with a scowl to Cargill's objections. He was a big, grim man, and his problem must have been to understand what Cargill was trying to say. His scowl transferred abruptly into an expression of astounded fury. "Well, I'll be darned," he said. "A Tweener trying to get out of marrying one of our girls—" Without warning, he launched a ham-like fist at Cargill's head.

Cargill ducked just in time to avoid the full impact of the blow. The huge fist seared along his cheek and sent him staggering across the room.

He came back, with narrowed eyes, body crouching low for the attack. From his left, Lela said sharply, "I'll sting your foot with this spitter. I'll burn you so you won't ever walk again. Don't you go starting a fight now."

The threat stopped Cargill. He had a tense conviction that Lela might actually have an impulse to lame him anyway. Then he'd never be able to get away.

"Sadie!" bellowed the minister. It was like a cue. A

small woman catapulted through the door and came up breathlessly.

"Yes, Henry," she said.

"Watch this Tweener scum," he said, "while Miss Lela and I"—he smiled knowingly—"make the arrangements. These forced Tweener weddings cost a little extra, you know." He and Lela went out of the room.

Cargill walked over to the window. Through the glass he could see the floater that had belonged to Carmean. It was less than a hundred feet away. "If I could get inside it," he thought, "I could be away from here in ten seconds." Unfortunately, Lela had taken the precaution of locking the door of the floater. He grew aware that the small woman had edged up beside him.

"I know something," she said in a loud whisper.

Cargill glanced at her, repelled by the avaricious look on her face and in her narrowed eyes. He said nothing.

Once more, the woman whispered hoarsely, "I heard the news on the radio this morning." She didn't wait for him to react to that, but rushed on eagerly, "What'll you give me if I tell the old man Carmean is against this wedding?"

The mystery of her demeanor was solved, and the implication it carried of this ministerial couple of the future was not pretty. He decided not to be critical. Hastily, he searched his pockets and held out the contents for her to look at. A pencil, a ball pen, a key ring with keys, some silver money, and his wallet.

The woman examined them with visible disappointment. "Is that all you got?" she asked. Suddenly, her face brightened. She reached over and touched his wrist watch. "What's that?"

Cargill unstrapped it and held it up to her ear. "It tells the time," he said. He wondered if it were possible that these people had no knowledge of watches. He couldn't remember if he had seen a timepiece aboard either the Bouvy floater or Carmean's ship.

The little woman looked disgusted. "I've heard of these things," she said, "but what good are they? The sun comes up in the morning and the sun goes down at night. That's good enough for me."

Cargill, who was learning fast, reached forward and took the watch from her fingers. "I can use it, if you can't," he said. "Now, I want you to tell me a couple of things."

"I'm not talking," said the woman.

"You'll talk," said Cargill, "or I'll tell your husband what I just gave you."

"You didn't give me anything."

"You can argue that out with him," said Cargill.

The woman hesitated, then said sullenly, "What do you want to know?"

"What did the radio say?"

The prospect of imparting information excited her. She leaned forward. "Carmean says you're to be caught. She says you're wanted by the Shadows. She says not to let any wedding take place." The woman's face twisted. "I never did like that woman," she said savagely. "If—" She stopped and drew away several paces.

Lela and the minister came back into the room. The girl was pale, the man angry.

"No deal," he said. "She won't pay me what it's worth."

"We'll live in sin," Lela said palely. "You've had your chance."

"You live in sin," retorted the minister, "and I'll bring the wrath down on your head."

Lela tugged at Cargill's arm. "He wanted me to change our ship for an old wreck he's got. Come on."

Cargill followed her, not quite sure how he should respond to what had just happened. He remembered his earlier thoughts about religion and "preachers," and, though this incident fitted, he was unwilling to let what he had just seen either affirm or decry his previous opinions. What was astonishing was that both Lela and "Henry" took the latter's ministerial powers for granted. Each accepted, somehow, that souls were involved, and that punishment was possible on the soul level. "Suppose," Cargill thought, "there *is* a soul, or at least that behind all the excitement of fifty thousand years of human soul-hunger, there is actual phenomena?"

It was hard to imagine that the reality had ever been more than vaguely glimpsed. People had been too rigid. All too frequently the vast powers of the state had been used to enforce an inflexible set of beliefs. And, where a breakaway was not a mere denial, the individuals somehow assumed they believed in a simple soul state-of-being. In connection with this, the word "immortal" was bandied about in such a loose fashion that it was instantly evident that no one had ever seriously thought about it.

The whole thing was disturbing because as a very concrete example of immortality, he had survived his normal death time by nearly four hundred years. Accordingly, for him the reality, or unreality, of the soul, or life force, or spirit, or whatever it might be, was more than just the academic thing it was to most people.

He was caught up in an astounding experience which surely involved all the actuality of the life process, the known and the unknown, including the hidden meaning behind the soul phenomena of ten thousand religions and a hundred thousand gods.

In one sense it was a mistake to think in terms of "soul," for such belief had a religious significance which automatically implied the belief was non-scientific, dependent on faith, incapable of being tested. Whereas, if there were phenomena, it would have manifested in innumerable ways, and would automatically be subject to laws. The fact that these laws might not be the same as those of the space-time continuum, known as the material universe, would not prevent them from being correlated in a scientific fashion.

"If," thought Cargill, as he entered the floater behind Lela, "I'm an energy field in the real universe, every time that field manifests itself somebody says 'Aha!' and we've got another philosophy."

He had a very strong conviction that it was a riddle he would have to resolve.

The days went by. Each morning their floater would drift up as high as its light-driven motor could carry them. On very clear, bright days that was as high as three miles. A thick mist could bring them down to within half a mile of the ground. And on a muggy or rainy day they had difficulty in clearing the higher hills. At such times, two or three hundred yards seemed to be their top altitude.

It was a strange, almost timeless existence, with nothing to do except watch the ground or lie on a cot and sleep, or sit in the all-room of the ship and plan escape.

Lela was the obstacle. It seemed to Cargill that he had never seen a girl so tense and wary. She slept in the control room, with the door locked. And yet, if he stirred, her light went on and he could see her watching him through the transparent door. That happened not just once, but every time. Her alertness baffled all his schemes. The end of this phase of their relationship came one night—Cargill wasn't sure whether it was the tenth or eleventh day since their escape; he had lost track of time.

As the floater settled to the grass beside a stream, he opened the outer door, stepped down and walked rapidly off among the trees. A muffled yell sounded from behind him. The beam of a powerful searchlight pierced the gathering twilight and silhouetted him in its glare. A hundred feet ahead of him a tree fell, seared and smoldering.

Cargill, who hadn't expected her to be able to fire at him from inside the control room, stopped short. Slowly, angrily, he returned to the ship. He had planned a showdown if he failed, and the moment had come.

Lela met him at the door, tense and furious. "You was trying to run away," she accused.

Cargill stopped and glared at her. "You bet I was. What do you think I'm made of—stone?"

His tone must have conveyed part of his meaning, for some of the anger faded out of the girl. Oddly enough, to some extent, the implication was true. As a single man in the army, he had learned not to be too discriminating about his girls. After eleven days alone with Lela, he no longer felt as critical of her. She had a youthful prettiness, and there was more than enough passion in her to satisfy any man.

But his purpose was more than conquest of a woman. He intended to take full control of the floater. He stared at her now, where she stood in the doorway, silhouetted against the light from inside. She held a spitter in her fingers; and that was his problem.

Boldly, he stepped closer to her. "It's one or the other," he said. "The two of us either live together here sensibly, or you'll have to kill me."

"Don't you come no nearer," said Lela, but her voice lacked conviction. She added, falteringly, "I've got to have marrying."

Cargill said urgently, "You know I've got to stick with you. Where else would I go?"

He stepped closer, so close that when she put up the

gun, the end of the tube touched his shirt. "I'm going to stay, but I won't be bossed, and I won't be put off."

Deliberately, he pushed against the gun. She started to back away. He reached out and caught her shoulders with his fingers. Ignoring the gun, he pulled her gently into his arms.

She was stiff and unbending. She kept mumbling something about "It's sin! It's sin!" Her lips when he kissed her trembled. She tried to pull away, and yet simultaneously her body went limp. She took the gun out from between them and held it off to one side, as if she were afraid it might go off. If ever a person was in a state of internal conflict, it was she.

"Give me the gun," said Cargill. "We've got to be equal. A woman has got to trust a man. It can't be any other way."

He kissed her again, and this time she offered no resistance. She was crying a little under her breath, a sound as old as the relationship between a man and a woman. Cargill instinctively kissed away her tears, and then reached over and took the gun.

Just for an instant, that made her stiffen; and then— and then she let him have it.

9

It seemed to Cargill that control of the sky floater would enable him to do what he wanted. But what did he want? The weeks passed and he could not make up his mind. For some reason he had become involved in a plot. If he made a move that brought him out into the open, the plotters would once more close in upon him, and would try to force him to do their will.

Finally, one day Cargill had an idea, the beginning of purpose. The nature of that purpose made him uneasy but the idea, once it came, would not go away. He went into the control room and sat down in front of the video plate. It was not the first time he had examined the machine or listened in to it. But now there was a plan in his mind.

As with the floater engine and other machinery, the TV and radio mechanism was completely enclosed, making it impossible for him to examine the inner workings of the instrument. For a while Cargill simply tuned into conversations and into the one program that was on.

A Shadow station broadcasted the program, which

consisted of popular music of the jive variety. After each selection, a persuasive voice urged the listener to come to Shadow City and receive Shadow training. To Cargill, who did not care for jazz, the "commercials" had been fascinating—in the beginning. Now he listened for a few moments to the repetitious music and then absently turned the dial.

Occasionally, he adjusted to see if any pictures were being broadcast. He found several. First, there was a man's coarse face and the man saying, "Now look, we've got to work this deal without any fooling." Cargill listened long enough to the "deal" to find out that it had to do with a boss bargaining as to how much he would receive for a new floater, which had been turned over to him by the Shadows. Cargill noted down the man's name, the details of the transaction and made another adjustment.

The next picture showed the interior of a ship. Apparently, a broadcaster had been left on carelessly. Since only the bosses had TV broadcasting units Cargill presumed that he was gazing into a boss's control room. He saw no one, though he watched for several minutes. A third picture featured a youth talking to a girl. He was saying, "Aw, c'mon, Jenny, you get your ma to put your floater down near ours tonight. Don't be one of these hard-to-get women."

There were other personal conversations. Cargill identified their nature and passed on. It was too early for the only television show broadcast by the Shadows. Not that he was any longer particularly interested in it. It always featured the arrival of Tweeners and Planiacs at the terminal center just outside Shadow City. Emphasis was given to the Planiacs. It was a man-in-the-street type of show in which a Shadow interrogator questioned new arrivals who wished to take Shadow training. When he had first heard the show Cargill had hoped the Shadows would actually picturize a part of their training program. So far they had not done so.

Not for the first time he felt disappointed that these receivers were unable to tune in on programs broadcast from Tweener cities. It was significant, of course. The Shadows were evidently making sure that no one else had the opportunity to control the floater folk.

Abruptly, Cargill shut off the instrument and sat frowning. His purpose, like a fire, threatened to consume him. And yet, once he took the plunge, he'd be even more of a marked man than he was now.

From the nearby control chair, Lela said anxiously, "What's the matter, honey?"

Cargill said slowly, "We can't go on like this forever —with everybody against us. We've got to have somebody around who will help us in an emergency or if something goes wrong."

Lela nodded uneasily, said reluctantly: "I've been thinking about that once in a while."

Cargill guessed that instead she had probably been making the effort not to think about it. Aloud, he said, "We've got to do more than think about it. We've got to do something."

"What, for instance?"

Cargill frowned. "There's one thing I've got to get straightened out first."

"What's that?"

"It's about something you told me once—which I can't quite believe anymore—about how many floater people there are. You said fifteen million."

She nodded, bright-eyed. "That's right. I wasn't fooling."

"Lela, it's impossible." He spoke urgently. "If there were that many people in the air, we'd be running into them continuously, every hour, every day, by the score."

The girl was silent. "It's a big country," she said at

last, stubbornly, "and I've heard Carmean and the other bosses of this area talking about it, and those are the figures they give. And, besides, you're not always looking out. I see lots of floaters, but I've been sort of trying to keep distance between us and them."

Cargill recalled her twenty-four-hour vigils in the control room and felt abruptly impressed. Remembering how tense she always was, he thought that perhaps he had underestimated the girl's perceptiveness. He still couldn't accept her figures, but he guessed that she just didn't have the information he wanted. His own estimate would be that there were fewer than five million Planiacs, perhaps not more than half that many. Cargill leaned back in his chair and closed his eyes. "Lela, what do people think of Carmean? Do they like her?"

It was a question which she would not actually be able to answer, since she couldn't know what millions of people thought. But people sometimes had extremely sensitive impressions. Lela said savagely, "Nobody likes Carmean. She's a skunk."

Cargill sighed but pressed on. "What about the other bosses? What do people think of them?"

"Why, you just put up with them," said Lela in a surprised tone. "There they are. They're part of life."

"I see," said Cargill, with satisfaction. She might not know it but her answer was more significant than any direct statement she might make. It reflected the beliefs and attitudes of a culture, the automatically accepted credos, the rigidities behind every thought and action. He opened his eyes and asked another question: "How did Carmean get to be a boss?"

"Just like any of the others, I guess," Lela said. "The Shadows started to give her things to give to the rest of us, and pretty soon we were all doing as she said to get our share."

Cargill nodded and asked, "And how did the Shadows come to pick up her?"

"Gosh, I don't know." Lela looked puzzled. "I never thought of that." She brightened. "I guess they looked her over and figured she had the stuff."

It was so superficial an answer that Cargill abandoned that line of questioning. He drew a deep breath and said, "Have you ever heard of a revolution?"

She hesitated, frowning. "You mean, where somebody starts a fight?"

Cargill smiled. "Something like that, but on a large scale. In the twentieth century, where I come from, we had possibly the most competent and determined revolutionists in the history of the world. Before they were even slowed down, they took over half the world. It took a long time for the rest of us to catch on to what they were doing, but finally it dawned on us, and we began to look into their methods."

There was a light of understanding in Lela's eyes. "You mean those Russes?" she asked.

Cargill agreed. "Yep, the Russes."

"They sure fixed those," said Lela.

Cargill, who had already heard how the fixing took place, did not pursue the subject. The great land mass had been divided into forty separate states. The fall of Sovietism produced a resurgence of religion on a singularly primitive level. It was a feudalistic disaster, product of the usual fears of a mentally sick hierarchy, uncreative, and so completely suppressive that the genius of half the people of earth had already been lost for two hundred years.

Cargill explained: "For us, the best thing to do would be to start off with a barrage of propaganda—and then wait to see what happens. The fight," he smiled grimly, "comes last." He turned back to the TV set, saying as he did so: "We'll take the first step right now."

By the fifth day of his broadcasts, Cargill began to have a queer feeling of unreality. He seemed to be talking into emptiness. For the first time in his life he understood how people must have felt in the early days of radio with only a microphone to stare at. What he lacked was a Hooper rating. There was no mail to bring an awareness of audience response, no surveys of any kind to encourage him. But in spite of his doubts he kept on.

Thirty days drifted by. On the morning of the thirty-first day, just as Cargill finished his propaganda talk, a man's face appeared on his TV plate. He was a cunning-looking individual about forty-five years old.

"I want to talk to you," he said.

A trap? Cargill's fingers hovered over the dial that would cut him off the air. He hesitated and the stranger had time to say, "My name is Guthrie. I want to talk to you about this rabble-rousing you've been doing."

He looked and sounded like a boss. He was a typical rough older Planiac and his words were sweet music to Cargill. But it was not yet time to talk.

"I'm not interested," said Cargill.

He broke the connection.

From that moment he began to name places where his supporters should meet and get together. It was dangerous but then so was being alive. What would save the great majority from counteraction was that each floater was armed with a mounted spit gun.

The days passed. Late one afternoon, Lela came briefly out of the control room. "It's going to be dark by the time we get to the lake," she said.

Cargill smiled. "Which lake do you mean?" He

added quickly, "Never mind. I'm just amazed constantly at the way you pick out these places."

"It isn't anything," said the girl. And she meant it. "I've been watching this country since I was a baby. I know it like the palm of my hand."

"Better, I'll wager," said Cargill.

They came in low over the trees and landed in a clearing with the aid of their searchlight. As Cargill started to open the door a spit gun flared in the darkness. What saved him was that he was behind the door. The energy spat past him and made a thunderous sound as it struck the metal corridor wall. The door smoked from the terrific heat. He had a sense of suffocation. Under him the ship began to lift. And then, once more, there was a sunlike glare—only this time the blow was delivered farther back, near the rear of the machine. The floater faltered and, as Cargill at last got the door shut, sagged back to the ground. It struck with a jar unlike anything that Cargill had ever experienced. He hurried to the control room and found Lela manning their spit gun.

She was very pale. "Those scum," she said, "have wrecked us."

The dawn light filtered through the turgid glass. It was dull at first, little more than a lighter shade of darkness, but it grew bright. From the control room Cargill could see the dark areas outside lightening. To his right was the gray horizon of the lake with the far shore hazed in mist.

From where she sat, manning the ship's powerful spit gun, Lela said, "It's bright enough now. Try and lift her again."

It was a hope that had motivated their courage all through the long night—that morning would bring some life to the sluggish motors. The hope died a second later as Cargill eased in the power and pulled it all the way back. The ship did not even stir.

"We'll try it again," said Lela in a tired voice, "when the sun comes up."

Cargill rejected her hope. "Has your father any influence with the bosses?" he asked.

The girl shrugged. "Carmean kind of likes him."

Cargill silently wondered why. He said finally, "Maybe if we talked to them we could find out what they want."

From the conversation he had heard more than a month ago between Carmean and the Shadow, Grannis, he had a rather sharp conviction they were after him.

He said, "I think you'd better try to get your Pa on the radio and see if he can come here. We'll try to hold them off until he arrives and then, if possible, you can go with him."

Lela was pale. "What about you?"

Cargill did not answer immediately. The feeling of vagueness that was inside him was only too familiar. It was the same kind of blur that had made it possible for him to run up a hill in Korea against enemy fire. With that blurred feeling about his future he had entered all battles in which he had been engaged. He said now, "I'll try to slip away tonight after it gets dark." He was about to elaborate when his gaze strayed past her toward the edge of the clearing a hundred feet away. A Shadow stood there.

Cargill's face must have shown that something was wrong, for Lela whirled. Her body grew rigid. The Shadow had been motionless as if observing the scene. Now he began to walk toward the ship. There was a dazed expression on Lela's face. She straightened slowly, settled herself behind the long spit gun and aimed it. Her face seemed bloodless and she sat very still. Twice she seemed in the act of pressing the activator of that remarkable weapon. Each time she shuddered and closed her eyes. "I can't," she whispered at last. "I *can't!*"

The Shadow was less than fifty feet away. With a frantic movement, Cargill pulled the girl out of the chair, settled into it and grabbed the gun. A sheet of flame reared up a dozen feet in front of the Shadow.

The Shadow paid no attention. He came on. Once more Cargill fired. The flame glazed through the Shadow. A score of feet behind him grass and shrubbery burned with a white intensity. Twice more Cargill fired directly into the Shadow shape—and each time it was as if there was nothing there, no resistance, no substance. And the Shadow came closer.

Cargill ceased firing. He was trembling. There was a thought in his mind—a new overpowering thought. If the Shadow shape were insubstantial, if potent, palpable energy meant nothing to it, then what about steel walls?

The next instant he had his answer. There was a blur of movement near the door, a swelling darkness. Lela screamed.

And then the Shadow was in the room.

10

Cargill had a blank awareness of getting out of the control chair and backing toward the far wall. The act of moving drained the initial sense of shock, and he stopped and stiffened. He saw that the Shadow shape had paused and was studying him. And, momentarily, he had time for another look at the strange phenomenon of . . . shadow.

In the dawn light that filtered into the room, the Shadow was a transparent, foggy structure, and that was what was so disturbing. This thing *had* structure. It should have flowed like any gaseous element until it had dissipated into formless mass. Instead, it was definitely human in silhouette.

He remembered his earlier speculations about the soul, and wondered: Is this it, somehow made visible? He couldn't quite accept that. A manifestation, perhaps, but even this idea seemed far-fetched and unsatisfactory. It was hard to believe that this was what had inspired five hundred centuries of humankind to a sense of spiritual ecstasy.

His evaluative thought ended abruptly, as the improbable creature spoke: "We meet again, Morton Cargill."

It was identification, not so much of Cargill, as of the Shadow. This must be the same Shadow he had seen with Ann Reece. Some of the others might have observed him while he was unconscious, but only one had *met* him.

Cargill's thought ended, and then he had no time for further immediate speculation. The Shadow said no more. He came striding forward. The foggy stuff that was his substance enveloped Cargill.

This time, there was no sense of transition. One instant he was in the floater with Lela and the Shadow. The next moment he was sitting in a chair, trying to blink away a blur over his vision. It cleared after several seconds and he looked around him.

He saw that he was in a chair at one end of a tastefully furnished living room. On one wall was a clock that said "May 6, 9:24 P.M." To his left was an open door through which he could see the edge of a bed.

The wall directly across from him was made of transparent glass and beyond it, at the far end of another room, he could see a girl sitting in a chair that seemed to be a replica of his own. Just for a moment, Cargill had the feeling that all this was strange and then he recognized the girl. He jerked erect with amazement.

It was the young woman who had tried to pretend that she was Marie Chanette.

He was back in the room where he had first arrived into the 24th century. And if the clock were right, then he was back to the evening of his original arrival.

He had actually no doubt about it. The knowledge grew out of a score of separate incidents that now drew together inside him to form the full perception: He had returned to the time of his arrival from the DREAM ROOM, from 1954.

Taking time to verify this idea, he trembled as he wrote a note to the girl and held it up against the glass. The note read: *How long have you been here?*

In answer, she wrote, *About three hours.*

Even though he expected something like that, the reply tensed Cargill. He told himself that he had to remember that she was capable of playing a devious game, and equally capable of lying. Several times during the past few months, he had considered this descendant of Marie Chanette, and her willingness to have him murdered as a part of her therapy.

He stood, eyes narrowed, fingers pressed against the transparent material that separated them, and stared at her. She also had been moved in time, back to 1954, then returned here. It made her as special as himself. It made it possible for him to ask himself: "What is there about her? How was the rigidity of time bypassed?"

It was an old question now for him, but the answer must be right here before his eyes, if only he could read the language in which it was written: The language of time-space, of reality, of the energy field that made up the complex of life. The language of eternity—perhaps. Cargill groaned inwardly and, closing his eyes, tried to recall at what exact moments in his own life there might have been manifestations which would now be meaningful. The blackouts, of course. Those highly charged moments when he had actually been transported through time. But they seemed unreachable, unanalyzable. There was the time when he had been wounded. Tensely, he remembered the shock as the bullet had struck him, the immediate numbness, and the sense of being far away.

Partial death? Cargill wondered. Just for a moment the feeling had come to him that his time had come. For many seconds, if there were such an energy field as he had conceived, the relationship between it and the physical structure that was Morton Cargill had been disturbed. And then, he'd realized that it was a minor injury. Almost immediately, the pain began, and the odd feeling of far-awayness ended.

It seemed like a clue to the search in which he—of all the people in the world—needed most to succeed. But it would have to wait. Distracted, he realized that this was not the time. It was theoretically possible that one person could resolve the riddle of the centuries in an hour. The decisive element would be the hypothesis with which one approached the subject. It was as true as ever that if one could ask the right questions, the right answers would be available. But at the moment he had to devote his attention to the urgent matter of a second escape.

He found himself wondering about Lela. What had happened to her? Or rather what *would* happen to her? He had to remember that what had happened was several months in the future. Staggered, he thought about some of the possible paradoxes.

The confusion that followed brought him out of his chair and sent him on a frantic exploration of the apartment. It was all as he remembered it and what was particularly important was that the bed looked as if he had previously slept on it. He remembered the chair that he had smashed, and raced from the bedroom back to the living room. He found the chair crumpled in a corner where he had tossed it. His picture of the limits of the paradox grew sharper. This was the room after Ann Reese had rescued him—not very long after, however.

Cargill began to sag. The pressure that was working on him was different from anything he had ever experienced. Different even from the first minutes of his initial arrival. There was a shattering implication here. If these people didn't like what had happened in any time period they could alter it. In one directed time-reversal they could cancel what had displeased them and the next time, with pre-knowledge, could force events to the pattern they desired.

It seemed clear that, after what he had done in trying to organize a Planiac rebellion, Grannis wanted the Shadows to carry through with their original purpose of murdering him. That would be the simplest way of nullifying the past.

His captors, knowing nothing of his months with the floater folk, could now proceed to kill him without ever suspecting that Grannis had plotted against them. Cargill decided grimly, "I'll fix that. The moment they get in touch with me I'll tell the whole story."

He was planning his exact words when a voice said from behind him, "Morton Cargill, it is my duty to prepare you for death."

The moment for action—and counteraction—had come. Cargill climbed to his feet. Fighting his anxiety and speaking clearly he launched into his account. He had time for half a dozen sentences and then the voice interrupted him, not deliberately, not with any intent to break into what he was saying. The interruption showed no awareness that he had said anything. Whoever was talking had not heard his words.

The voice said, "Events are supremely convincing. I shall now describe to you the complex problem with which you presented us when Marie Chanette was killed in the twentieth century."

Cargill couldn't help it. He had to cut in. He said loudly, "Just a minute. You've explained this to me before."

"Violence," the voice said, "affects not just one individual but future generations as well."

Cargill shouted, "Listen to me. There's a plot—"

"It's like a stone," said the voice, "that is flung furiously into a limitless sea. The ripples go on forever and wash up many a strange flotsam on shores remote beyond imagination."

Cargill trembled with anger. "You stupid idiots!" he yelled. "Surely you haven't put me in here without any chance of telling you what's happened." But his very anger measured the extent of his own belief that this was exactly what they had done.

Inexorably, the voice continued. And for the first time Cargill realized that it was giving him information different from that of—months ago. "Listen to the case," it said, "of Marie Chanette."

For better or worse he listened. His muscles tensed and his mind jumped with impatience, but he listened. Gradually then, in spite of his own purposes, he grew calmer and began to feel fascinated.

Much indeed had happened as the result of the death of Marie Chanette. She died in a car accident and in pain. The pain ended with her death but that was not the end. There was no normal end.

Marie Chanette was survived by a daughter who, at the time of her mother's decease, was three years and two months of age, and by a husband from whom she was not yet officially divorced. The fight for the possession of the child had been bitter and on the death of her mother, little Julia Marie reverted automatically to the care of her father, an insurance salesman.

At first he kept her in a nursery school and had a neighboring woman tend her after the school bus brought her home. At first he spent occasional evenings with her. But he was a hard worker, and evening calls on prospects were part of his routine. The enforced habit of not having much to do with his daughter made it easy to forget all about her on evenings when it was just a matter of going out with the gang for a good time. He told himself that she was really getting a better upbringing than if her mother had been alive and that he was "paying plenty" for her care. When Julia Marie asked why she didn't have a "mummy" like the other kids he decided in her own interests (so he informed himself) to tell her his distorted version of the truth.

He discovered, however, that she already knew it. Some of the other kids had heard garbled stories and had shrieked the words at her. These tales were locked up tightly inside her heart. She grew up unstable, blotchy-faced, easily upset, a bad-tempered, wilful child —"just like your mother, blast you!" Chanette shouted at her when he was drunk.

She never got over the tensions of her childhood, though she turned out to be a good-looking girl and had a brief exciting spring between the ages of 21 and 25. She married in 1973 a young man named Thompson, who was not good enough for her. But she had too great a negation of self to aspire to anything higher. In 1982 she gave him a boy child, a girl in 1984. She died in 1988, ostensibly from a major hysterectomy but actually from an ultimate case of overwrought nerves.

Thompson drifted along for a while at his job but now that the intense, driving, frightening personality of his wife was no longer pushing him he was quick to retreat from responsibility. He lacked the capacity to appreciate the benefits he had accumulated in fifteen years of service with the Atomotor Corporation. Just as he was about to be promoted to the kind of field work which the firm's "Constitutional" psychologist had recommended for him, he traded his atobout for a floater, gave up his job, sold his house—and became a Planiac.

They called them that in those lazy glorious days just before the turn of the twenty-first century. They were floaters, people who had no home but a house in the sky. All day long they floated through the air anywhere from a few thousand feet to a few miles up. At night they would come down beside a stream and cast for fish. Or they would float down onto the ocean and return to land with a catch which some cannery would be glad to buy. They followed the crops. They were the new race of fruit pickers, harvesters and casual laborers. They remained a day, a week, but seldom a month. They only wanted a stake, enough money to live until tomorrow.

In 2010 A.D. it was estimated that nineteen million people in the United States had become floaters or Planiacs. The stay-at-home majority was shocked and economists predicted disaster for the land unless something was done to bring the skyriding population back to earth. When a hard-pressed Congress in 2012 tried to pass a law restricting sky-riding to vacations only, it was too late. The voting power of the Planiacs frightened the house majority, and thereafter the floaters—who had themselves received a big scare—were a political force to be reckoned with.

The bitter feeling between the floaters and the grounders, already intense, grew sharper and deadlier with the passing years. Everyone took sides. Some who had been grounders bought floaters and joined the restless throngs in the sky. Others, vaguely recognizing the danger and moved by some kind of moral feeling, descended from the sky.

Among the latter was an oldster named William Thompson, his grown-up son, Pinkey, and his daughter, Christina. Pinkey Thompson never married and so he was merely an environment, a ne'er-do-well anthropological "climate," an irritant on the slime of time. He existed, therefore he influenced those with whom he came in contact. Whatever he took into his cells before severing bodily connection with his mother manifested indirectly. Many years were to pass before psychologists proved that the tensions of men too could affect the child. But Pinkey had no child.

When Christina Thompson, his sister, came out of the blue sky her grandmother, Marie Chanette, had been dead sixty-one years. The emotional ripples of her death had therefore already reached into another century. Her mother's tense body had precipitated Christina into life in the eighth month of her pregnancy. The seventh month would have been better. During the eighth month certain growths occur in a child which should not be disturbed.

The process was disturbed in Christina. She was a quiet intense little girl, given to sudden, unexpected tears and when she was younger was a problem to her father and brother. She knew, in a casual fashion, about the way her grandmother had died.

What she did not know was that the new psychology had already established that people could be affected by events in the remote past of the continuous protoplasm which had passed from mother through daughter since the first cell divided in two. Christina reluctantly attached herself to a job and, when she was twenty-eight, married the son of a former Planiac. The three children that arrived in quick succession were demoralized by the endless plans of their restless poverty-stricken parents to save so they could buy a floater, so that they could forever abandon the hardships of ground life. Two of the children dreamed with their parents but the second child, a girl, reacted violently against what she came to consider her parents' shiftless attitude. Their very talk made her uneasy and insecure.

Her opinions being discovered she became unpopular until she learned to show false enthusiasm for the venture. She ran away when she was eighteen, on the eve of the first trip in the hard-earned floater.

She had several jobs, then at twenty-one she became a clerk in a small air-transport company. Small! It barely paid a living wage to the father and son who owned it, in addition to paying her salary. When she married Garry Lane, the son, at twenty-two, it looked like a very poor match, even to her desperate eyes. But it was a love match and, surprisingly, the business prospered.

It was not exactly surprising—the son had a personality. When he made a contact it held. Business flew their way and soon they lived in a grand house. They had two children, Betty and Jack. And what saddened the parents was that both were highly disturbed individuals. Specially trained nurses were hired, but they did not help as much as the parents hoped.

At twenty-four Betty Lane, having been advised that her instability was not rooted in her own childhood, was directed by her personal psychologist to go to the Inter-Time Society for Psychological Adjustment. She went. An investigation was made and it was decided that the death of Marie Chanette was responsible.

"—and that," said the voice from the air in front of Cargill, "explains why you are here in this therapy room. Tomorrow morning it will be necessary to kill you in order that the effects of Marie Chanette's violent death can be nullified. That is all."

There was silence and it was evident that the speaker had withdrawn.

For an hour Cargill paced the room, his temper steadily gathering strength. Incredibly the Shadows, despite their vaunted superiority, were going to be destroyed by the schemes of one of their number. It served them right, Cargill told himself in fury. Imagine setting up a situation whereby their victims couldn't even talk to them—the silly, stupid fools!

In renewed rebellion against his fate, he again ex-

plored the apartment. First the living room and then—
As he entered the bedroom, Ann Reece was just getting
up from the floor. She saw him and put a finger to her
lips. "Ssssshh!" she said.

Cargill blinked at her with eyes that watered with
relief. He could have rushed over and hugged her. He
had to restrain himself from racing over to the elongated
tube-like instrument which had brought her, grabbing at
it and shouting, "Let's get out of here!" He restrained
himself because it was up to her to show if she remembered a previous rescue.

She said, "This time let's not waste a moment. It's
bad enough having to come twice."

This time—twice! That was all he wanted to know.
Silently, sure of himself again, Cargill grabbed at the
tube. He blinked—and it must have happened as
quickly as that.

11

He was standing on a dusty road and it was quite dark. A few feet from him Ann Reece was bent over, making adjustments to the long tube-like transport instrument. She had evidently recovered more quickly than he.

She looked up and said satirically, "Well, here we are, starting all over again, Mr. Cargill."

Briefly her sarcastic tone blurred the implication of what she had said. And then he thought shakily that somewhere around here, just about this time of day and possibly on this very day, he had run off into the brush. At this very moment, about a mile from here, Lela and her father were settling down beside a lake, and in a few moments she would capture Morton Cargill number one. He had an impulse to escape again and watch that other Morton Cargill's capture. He shook his head, rejecting the desire. A man threatened as he was had no time for side excursions.

Ann Reece lifted the transporter and said to somebody behind Cargill, "All right, Lauer, you take this back to Grannis."

A young man stepped past Cargill. In the darkness it

was almost impossible to see him. He said sourly, "I don't see why we want to give it back to him. We haven't got anything like this."

Ann Reece shoved the transporter into his hands, grabbed him by the arm and led him along the road out of hearing. Cargill could see them only vaguely. They were arguing furiously. Presently Lauer must have yielded for he shouldered the instrument and trudged off. Ann came back to Cargill .

"We wait here," she said, "and this time you'd better not try to run off." She added to somebody in back of him, "If he makes a break spit him."

Cargill had heard the men behind him but he hadn't looked at them and he didn't intend to. The quarrel between Lauer and Ann interested him. It implied that some Tweeners at least were dissatisfied with Grannis. He wondered idly if he might not be able to lay the groundwork for another revolution.

The minutes trickled by. In the nearby brush a nightbird trilled, breaking the intense silence. Far away a coyote howled mournfully. Cargill felt a sudden press of air against him as if a big bird had passed over his head on silent wings. Beside him Ann Reece's flashlight blinked on. She pointed it into the sky, waved it violently, then turned to Cargill.

"In a few minutes," she said, "a volor will come down here. Don't say a word, just get in and go to the rear away from the pilots." She added in a low tone, "The air transport men are anxious to get hold of you. They want to question you about the air fighting in the twentieth century. But they can't have you till you've been trained."

Cargill, who had been an Infantry officer, maintained a discreet silence.

"Sssshh," said Ann Reece unnecessarily, "here they come."

The machine that settled down toward them over the trees was not a floater. It had swept-back wings and a long metal body. It must have been made of superstrong alloys for it crushed down among the trees that lined the narrow roadside and snapped one bole with a casualness that was all the more impressive by the roar with which the tree fell. There was a rush of wind and then the plane slowed for the landing and poked a bright beam of light at them. A side door opened. Cargill ran forward, aware of the young woman following close behind. The entrance was higher than it had looked from a distance, and he had to scramble to get inside. Slipping past a man in uniform, who was coming forward, he fumbled his way along a dimly lighted aisle, and finally sank into the seat farthest to the rear.

He heard Ann Reece say, "Help me up!"

The young man said something Cargill couldn't hear, but it had ancient connotations.

Ann Reece snapped, "Let go of my hand. I can hold it myself, thank you."

The officer laughed, then said, "Was that the great man?"

Cargill heard no more. The machine moved, slowly at first, then with a violence that left no doubt as to how different it was from the slow-motion floaters which —as Cargill knew only too well—were practically helpless at night.

It climbed steeply, like a plane rather than an airship. And its speed after less than a minute was something to murmur about. He couldn't remember ever having been in a machine that moved so fast. It gave him pause and made his purpose seem less than possible. People who could build such planes had an advanced mechanical culture, and they would not be easily controlled by a man from the twentieth century. His partial success with the floater folk must have gone to his head. He was setting himself against people who were actually planning an attack against the mysterious Shadows.

The self-negation did not end until he suddenly remembered that these people thought he was important. He could not fully reject their opinion. The fact that they held it at all would give him contacts normally unavailable to a person coming into a new environment.

He would learn what they thought. Minority groups would take his presence into account. Plans might be altered on the basis of things that he said.

It would be vital for him to become oriented to the entire Tweener situation as quickly as possible, so that he could start to make sensible plans of his own. The possibilities cheered him. He turned his attention back to the flight itself. Somehow, he expected it to end momentarily, but the minutes drifted by, and still the rapid flight continued.

He was aware that Ann Reece had seated herself several seats ahead of him, but he had no impulse to join her. A whole hour went by, by his watch.

The city came suddenly out of the distance. Great bulbs of light floated in the sky and glared down on the buildings below, vividly lighting up the scene. Ann Reece settled into the adjoining seat, but Cargill scarcely noticed.

It was a city of skyscrapers that sparkled at him from the distance with effervescent, changing lights. Seeming to be made of glass, the buildings' translucent opalescence glowed softly. The first feeling of alienness passed. Cargill gazed at the city, excitement quickening his pulse.

Beside him Ann Reece said quietly, "You're the first outsider in twenty years to see the capital."

Cargill looked at her questioningly. "You mean no strangers are allowed in Tweener territory?"

Ann Reece shook her head. "This is our capital city," she said. "It contains all the secrets of our people. We cannot afford to take chances. For twenty years all new Tweeners, all Tweeners who have failed in the Shadow tests, have been sent to other cities. No Shadow, not even Grannis, has been permitted to enter in that time."

"How can you stop the Shadows?" Cargill asked. He was remembering the way Grannis had walked unharmed through the fire of the spit gun that he had directed from Lela's and his floater.

"They're not as invulnerable as they would like us to believe," said Ann Reece, a grim note in her voice. "If you concentrate enough fire on them they run as fast as any ordinary mortal. We've discovered that." In the darkness inside the volor, she made a gesture he didn't see. She added: "Anyway we don't permit them to enter our territory. We are very strict about that. No one can enter the areas under our control without permission, and everyone who does enter has to submit to a thorough investigation."

"How much of this continent do you control?" Cargill asked.

"About one quarter."

Cargill nodded. He remembered how many times Lela had turned the floater aside, and said, "That's Tweener territory. We don't go there." He nodded again, half to himself. The floater folk must have discovered through experience that Tweener territory was dangerous.

"And where's Shadow City?" he asked.

"Oh, that's in the Rockies. The city is an impregnable fortress, hewn out of the rocks of an almost inaccessible mountain and protected by an energy screen. It's approachable only by air."

They were over the Tweener capital now. Cargill had a glimpse of a series of glittering shopping centers.

Gradually the streets below became more residential in nature. The volor began to slant down. He saw that it headed toward a broad expanse of lawn, which evidently belonged to an estate. In the distance he saw what looked like stone fences. A large house stood well back among the trees.

Ann Reece said, "This is my home."

Cargill looked at her in surprise. Then he looked at the house and whistled softly unnder his breath. He had taken it for granted that Ann Reece was merely a minor agent, an unimportant cog in this affair.

Alighting from the volor, he looked again at the house. It was spacious and beautiful. It was of stone and its walls rose in ever higher peaks and spires until, like those of some dimly seen dream-castle, they faded from sight in the high shadows. The windows were tall and pointed at the tops, and the door huge and matching the windows in design. Broad white steps led to the house proper. Truly an estate, he thought with a quick intake of breath. Such a house, he estimated, would have cost three or four hundred thousand dollars in Los Angeles, 1954.

He climbed the steps wonderingly. It was evident that in this environment he would indeed be moving in high Tweener circles. Ann Reece rang the bell. There was a pause and then the door was opened by an elderly man.

The man said, "Welcome home, Miss Reece."

"Thank you, Granger," said Ann. She motioned Cargill to go past her, and they walked silently along a brightly lighted corridor and came presently to a room.

Cargill noted that it was large and well furnished. Directly across from him were a series of French doors that led to a terrace. Without hesitation he strode towards the doors and, trying one of them, was surprised to find it open.

He had intended only to glance out, to gain a quick

view of his surroundings. What he saw snatched his attention. The city—seen for the first time from the ground. When Ann Reece and he had arrived at the house, the volor had landed them almost at the door. There had been little chance to observe the great globes of light that floated above the city. Seen from the air, from the tremendously swift volor, the globes had appeared stationary. Now he saw that they were moving steadily like the stars in their courses. They shed their light like miniature suns on the metropolis below and followed each other in a great circular movement.

Wearily, Cargill turned away. As he walked slowly back into the room, he realized how tired he was. It had been a long waking period, beginning with the normal day with Lela, and then followed by the long tense night while the floater was under seige. There had been periods of sharp fear, and periods of hopelessness, and periods of rage—all of them exhausting. And that was only the beginning. Back in the Shadow prison, he had for a sustained period faced the prolonged anxiety induced by the threat of death for some fantastic therapy. This was followed by more strain. The rescue by Ann Reece had brought relief from one fear, but it had not brought an end to physical activity. And so, for two hours more, there had been a further drain on his strength.

He saw that the girl was studying his face. She said after a moment, matter-of-factly: "I'll have some food prepared for you. And then you can go to bed. I imagine you can use it."

Cargill wasn't hungry, but it occurred to him that he hadn't eaten for twenty-four hours, and maybe he'd better have something. Ann Reece was turning away when Cargill remembered something. "I've been intending to ask you," he said. "What happened to you after I escaped that first time?"

"I reported your escape to Grannis, naturally. About half an hour later there was a time adjustment and I had to do the job again."

"Half—an—hour—later?" said Cargill.

He stared at her, more startled then he cared to admit. His picture of the process of time manipulation had been vague. Suddenly he saw it as something that was done to one individual. She hadn't lived those months. For her the adjustment had taken place this very first night. Those who controlled the time stream really had potent power over its flow.

It didn't seem to occur to Ann Reece to ask what had happened to him. She moved to a door and disappeared.

Cargill was served a thick steak, medium rare, a baked potato and for dessert a baked apple. He ate with a concentration and purpose that reminded him of his first meal aboard the Bouvy floater. Thought of Lela made him feel tense. And so, when he suddenly looked up and saw that Ann was sitting back, watching him with amusement, it irritated him. She had changed her dress while the meal was being prepared. The short skirt was gone and she wore a long blue gown that matched the color of her eyes. It also made her look much younger. She had a pert face on which she wore a faintly calculating expression. Her lips were firm and well-shaped, and she carried herself with an air of great assurance.

"What's all this about?" Cargill said. "What are you going to train me for?"

Her expression changed. A set look came into her eyes and her lips tightened. But her voice retained some of the humor of her earlier amusement. She said, "You're the key figure. Without you there's no war."

"I'm sure I'm thrilled," said Cargill acridly. "Does that make me a general?"

"Not exactly." She broke off, snapped: "We're sick of the horrible world the Shadows have created for us." Her voice had lost its lightness. It was hard with anger. She flared: "Imagine changing the past, so that people will gradually become more civilized, get over their neuroses, and all that nonsense. It's against reason, against—religion."

"Religion?" said Cargill, remembering his own speculations. "Do you believe in the soul?"

"God is within everyone," she said.

Cargill had heard that one before. "People keep saying that," he said, "but then they act as if they don't mean it. *Let's just assume for a moment that it's true.*"

"Of course it's true." She was impatient. "What do you mean, assume?"

"I mean," said Cargill, "let's assume it as a scientific fact."

She was silent. A wary expression came into her face. Cargill knew that look. He had seen it in the eyes of the chaplain of his company, and in the faces of other people whenever the subject of their belief was pressed too hard.

"Scientific?" she said, and she made it a term of opprobrium.

Cargill laughed. He couldn't help it. Her house was filled with "scientific" equipment. She had rescued him by the use of scientifically developed mechanisms that impressed even him, who came from a scientifically oriented world. But now he had applied the term to a forbidden area of thought.

He ceased his laughter with an effort, and said soberly: "I'm honestly beginning to believe that I'm the only person who really thinks the soul might exist. My picture of it is perhaps a little more wonderful than that of even those who give lip service to the word and to the idea behind it. At first, I thought it might be an energy field in space-time, but that doesn't quite take into account the vast age of the material universe. The way I've been moved around makes time curiously unimportant as a factor. It would be easy, on the basis of the estimated age of the universe, to make all religions look ridiculous, but that isn't what I want to do. I'm guessing that all this smoke has a hot fire under it somewhere, but the understanding we've had so far is just a superficial glimpse at the underlying reality. What do you think of that?"

"I really don't care to discuss the matter, Mr. Cargill." She was cold. "Your childish speculations are not exactly an insult, since you do seem sincere; but they ignore a thousand years of religious thought."

"You mean," said Cargill, "ten thousand years of making the effort not to know, of belief enforced by just such an attitude—and never a good look at what might actually be there. Well, I'll take the look myself and I'll keep you in touch."

Ann Reece smiled grimly. "You won't have much time for private speculations. You'll be too busy helping us change our world."

Cargill studied her from under narrowed eyelids. The reminder that he was to be used in their plans abruptly enraged him. "This world of yours," he said, "does it include justice for individuals?"

Her lips were clenched into a thin line. "There's only one way to change the world," she said slowly. "We've got to get rid of the Shadows, and force the Planiacs out of the sky to a life of usefulness. Once that happens, it won't be long before this planet is humming again with industry and all that makes life worth living. Henceforth, justice will always include hard work."

Cargill glanced deliberately around the luxuriously furnished room. "For you, also?" he asked, softly.

She must have caught the implication, for she flushed.

She said, "Your idea that people who manage estates don't work at it is just not so."

It was true, of course, in an important sense. But he felt too basically hostile to her to be impressed by her vision. He said, "But where do I fit into this? What is the training that I'm to be given?"

12

Ann Reece relaxed. The amused look came back to her face. She said with heavy irony, "One times one times one times one times zero equals a million. That's the mathematics involved in your training. Anything else you want to know?"

"Damn you!" said Cargill. He was on his feet, leaning over the table toward her. "If you people expect any cooperation from me you'd better start telling me the facts. Whose idea was it to use me in whatever you plan to use me for in this Shadow City attack?"

"Grannis'."

That held him briefly. "How come," said Cargill finally, "that you're all playing the game of a Shadow traitor?"

Ann Reece was cool. "We're not playing his game. He's playing ours. He agrees with us. He thinks we have the answer to the problems of this age."

"You fools!" Cargill was scathing. "Why, you're just a bunch of babes in the wood—"

He stopped himself in alarm. Careful, he thought. This was no time to reveal his knowledge that Grannis was playing on several sides. Slowly he settled back into his chair. He stared at her unsmilingly. She said, "As soon as you've finished eating I'll show you to your bedroom. You sound tired." There was no doubt of the sarcasm in her voice.

After she had left him Cargill explored his bedroom. The walls were done in shades of green, contrasting very effectively with a vividly white bed and white furniture.

He was surprised when he looked out of the window, to see that the room was on the second floor. Since he had climbed no stairs he guessed that the house was built on the side of a hill. He mentally measured the distance to the ground below, then frowned with irritation. Twenty feet was a considerable drop even for a strong active man. Not that it mattered. He doubted that he'd get far if he tried to escape through the window. He realized his method of handling this situation must be on a much higher level of action.

He turned back into the room and started to undress. He was tired and he fell asleep almost immediately.

Even as he slept he became aware of a voice talking to him, urging him to action. It said something about Shadow City and the necessity of breaking down the Shadow pyramid. "Throw the switch," the voice commanded. "And the signal for you to act is—is—"

It faded away. The sound and its echoes retreated into an abyss of time and space. He grew aware that Ann Reece and a man were in the room. The man said: "Does that complete it?"

"That completes it," said Ann Reece.

The two of them went out.

Cargill waited for he knew not what. Whatever had happened didn't feel complete inside him. He had the strange sensation that something basic at the heart of his being had been disturbed. "It's because of the thoughts I've had about reality," he decided. "Except for that—it would be complete."

A geometrical design drifted past his inner eye. It had black areas in it; and there must have been grief emotion, for he felt suddenly depressed. The interesting thing was that he knew what the design meant. It was a fold in the time continuum. Even as he watched it, tensely, it altered almost imperceptibly. Various lines, like threads of a fabric, seemed to fray, and he had the uneasy feeling that something was being strained almost to breaking. It remained poised in delicate and dangerous balance.

The picture in his mind's eye changed and became a scene. He seemed to be on a hill overlooking a lake that glittered at him with radioactive fluorescence. Except for the fiery blue lake, as far as he could see to every horizon was desolation. Without knowing where the knowledge came from, Cargill knew that the lake was a life-discard, dropped on the track of time countless billions of years earlier.

What was more interesting about his awareness was the distinct conviction that the lake was an experiment which he had started personally, and abandoned. The lake, thus casually treated, clung to its "life," and had maintained itself for almost the full period of the existence of the material universe. At the moment, it was in communication with another life-discard on the planet of a remote star. The communication was a kind of regeneration process whereby each furnished the other with energy elements essential to survival. The intricate interrelationship had strong love characteristics.

Cargill watched the lake briefly, tuned in on the telepathy, and then—without effort—crossed the void to where the other being existed. Here were craggy mountains, a plantless, treeless horizon of gray-brown soil; and high on a mountain peak was a giant statue. The statue was a dead black in color and had no resemblance to a human shape. And yet, Cargill knew, it was a try at form, an attempt to achieve life on a higher level than the lake.

The idea of life that moved had not yet entered his thought. He himself did not move, as movement. There was no space, except what he imagined, and only the lake and the statue had time in them. It was a brilliant creative process, as he had originally conceived it. By imagining space, by having a high wave and low wave concept of space (thus setting up energy flows), by enforcing an energy slow-down to the point where it took on the appearance of matter, he deluded the lake and the statue into believing that they *were* something and *possessed* something. Thereafter, they fought desperately to sustain the illusion. It took up so much of their "energy" that they didn't have "time" to examine any other reality.

The scene began to fade. He had a tendency to hold onto it, but he realized the pictures were a chance contact with an ancient memory, and important only in that a rigidity in his present beingness had been overcome; it signified that for a moment he had been free. He guessed, without having any detail, that there would be millions of scenes like that . . . elsewhere.

He seemed to be back in the bed, and he was about to settle into a warm comfortable sleep when the realization dawned: He was not yet complete. The feeling of imbalance remained. He saw the geometric design again, and it looked less dangerous—the threads seemed not so frayed, the fabric appeared firmer. Except that it moved.

As he watched, it swayed and wavered as if it were being blindly, fumblingly probed.

His first fleeting awareness of something more concrete was of cool sheets and the clean, antiseptic smell of a hospital. He awakened as from a deep sleep, but with a total awareness of physical well-being that was startling. He lay motionless, with eyes closed, becoming aware of the unfamiliar sensation—a joy of being alive, he thought. He felt delighted that it could be so.

He knew without particularly thinking about it that this was not the bedroom in Ann Reece's home. All that seemed far away, though not so far as a few minutes before . . . with the lake. That had been truly remote. This was—he couldn't decide.

He was puzzling over the different feeling that this had, when a woman spoke. "How much longer?" she asked.

It was not the voice of Ann Reece; and that was—so it seemed at first—what made him keep his eyes shut.

Footsteps sounded on a carpeted floor, and then a pleasant baritone voice replied: "I'll call you when he wakes. After all, we took advantage of an opportunity here. Everything had to be spontaneously done without preliminary thought."

Her answer seemed pettish. "Shouldn't our control of time have made it possible for us to do this better?"

The man remained respectful but firm. "We don't have control beyond the second fold. The gap between our present era of 7301 A.D. and the twenty-fourth century is so vast that—"

She cut him off. "I am familiar with these arguments. Notify me the instant he recovers."

Cargill had the impression that she moved away, and he took the opportunity to cautiously slit one eyelid open. He closed it again immediately, but he had had a quick glimpse of a scantily arrayed woman pausing at a doorway and looking back. He had a dimmer impression that she had a cape thrown back over one shoulder. Evidently, she had paused for an anti-climactic remark, for she spoke again:

"I feel uneasy about all this," she said, "as if everything is somehow out of our control."

"Madam, this will continue to be true for some time to come."

Cargill opened both his eyes slightly at that point, and cautiously kept them open. He saw that the woman was dressed in a bra that resembled what sometimes accompanied a bathing suit in the 1950's, and that her dark blue shorts gave a similar impression of belonging to the beach, or at least suggested that the climate was sub-tropical. She had an ankle-length cape of metallic gold net flung over her right shoulder. Her dark hair shimmered with a faint bluish light and framed a face with high cheekbones and deep-set eyes. It was not a beautiful face but it was a distinctive, aristocratic one. It implied race pride, family pride, pride of position.

Even as he looked at the woman, Cargill saw out of the corner of one eye that a gray-haired man with a young face was watching him with a guarded air that indicated consternation. Cargill somehow got the idea that he should pretend unconsciousness until after the woman departed. He started to sigh with resignation but caught himself in time and quietly closed his eyes. The woman must have chosen that moment to leave the room, for when he peeped again, she was in the act of walking through the open door. She did not look back.

The man carefully closed the door and then came over to the side of the high, hospital-type bed. Giving Cargill a long, searching look, he seemed satisfied with what he saw, for he said with an understanding smile: "I'm Lan Bruch"—he pronounced it "brooch"—"and I want to assure you that you are in no danger. All your questions will be answered soon." He adjusted the dials of a small box on the table beside the bed.

Instantly, Cargill's feeling of eager impatience was replaced by a comfortable lethargy. He yawned and closed his eyes.

When he awakened the next time, the feeling of well-being seemed even greater than the first time. With it came a tremendous urge for action; he sprang straight over the foot of the bed, and landed in the center of the room with all the poise and grace of an acrobat. The leap astonished him. He had had the fleeting thought that he would like to do it, and the thought had been instantly converted into motion.

He glanced down. He was naked and the tanned, smooth-muscled body he saw was certainly not his. A tiled bathroom adjoined the bedroom. He strode into it and studied the face in the mirror. At first, he decided it was not his. And then, he couldn't be sure. He certainly seemed younger, more serene; the countenance that stared back at him resembled those in certain touched-up photographs he had had taken years before.

Cargill showered rapidly, not entirely displeased, and only casually concerned about what had happened to him. He looked around presently for shaving materials, but finding none suddenly knew that he didn't have to shave, and also he had the odd sensation that he wouldn't even know how to shave. That startled him again. But the man had said he would explain everything.

As Cargill emerged from the bathroom, Bruch came through the door from the hallway. He carried a toga-like raiment which he handed to Cargill, who examined it curiously. Then, since it was a simple enough design, he slipped it on. An ornamented cord fastened neatly around the waist, fitting the garment snugly against his skin. As he emerged from the bathroom—where he had gone to dress—Cargill saw that Lan Bruch had seated himself at a table near a window that had been curtained until this moment. It had been so cunningly curtained, indeed, he hadn't even noticed. He strode to the window in his flamboyant fashion, and felt immediately amazed. The window was ablaze with sunlight, but all around were mountain peaks. Below a mass of clouds he could vaguely make out the outlines of buildings.

From behind him, Bruch said: "Sit down. Have some breakfast. Enjoy the view."

Cargill turned automatically. Magically, the table had opened up. Steaming dishes were spread on its glittering surface. Two cups of what looked like coffee were already poured. A pitcher of cream, sugar, familiar tableware made the scene normal. Cargill seated himself, sniffed happily at the coffee, and put in his normal complement of cream. Across the table from him, Bruch said:

"Just in case you're wondering, that's not Shadow City out there. It's Merlic, the capital city of Merlica. The year is 7301. You were brought here because we need your help and cooperation. As soon as you understand the situation you will be returned to the Tweener capital, and events will proceed as before, except that we hope you will understand that it is absolutely vital that the Tweeners be victorious over the Shadows."

He held up his hand, as Cargill made to interrupt. "Wait! Let me give you the facts in my own way. What the Shadows started in the twenty-second or twenty-third century had more implications than they realized. A civilization which would not normally have existed came into partial existence as a result of their work, and it has never quite become real. See that city down there—" He motioned at the mist below—"It's not really there yet. If you were to go down into it, you would find yourself coming presently to what is literally the edge of the world.

"You, being more real than I, would probably be disturbed by it. I accept my tentative existence but I am very determined to make it real. You may ask, how can such a thing be? To begin with, I won't go into all the laws governing time. They're very complex, and to understand them would require a long period of conditioning—"

Cargill silently disagreed. Whatever its value, his experience with the lake and the statue had given him an understanding of time that was not complex at all. You gave life-energy something to hold onto, and as soon as it started to cling and maintain and hold, *there* was time. Time was *havingness*. In handing the material universe the life-energy to hold onto, time had literally been created in the process. He didn't have to imagine how rigid that holding could be. He had lived it.

Lan Bruch was continuing: "We have a fairly solid pattern of existence up to about the Shadow-Tweener war. At that point we have a fold, or a fault, or a flaw in the time-space continuum; and if anything goes on after that, we can't make contact with it. Captain, we've got to make Merlica real, and so establish a solid reality for this planet from the twenty-fourth century up to present time. This can only be done if the Tweeners win the war."

Cargill glanced again out of the window at the clouds and the mountain peaks and the vaguely visible city. He shook his head, wonderingly, thinking: "They evidently haven't anything to hold onto as yet." Aloud, he said: "Just what do I have to do to insure the Tweener victory?"

An amazing thing happened. He could see Lan Bruch's lips move, as the man replied. But he heard no sound. He leaned forward, straining. But the scene itself was fading. The table, and Bruch himself, and the room seemed to turn into mist that wavered and twisted—and darkened. In a flash, then, all was gone.

He was back in a bed. Only this time he knew it was the bed at Ann Reece's home. Cargill awakened with a start, and simultaneously realized three things: It was broad daylight; it *was* the bedroom in the Tweener capital, and a voice was saying from the air just above his head: "The signal for you to act will be the phrase: *'Visit us some time.'*"

He felt briefly confused. Had all this been a dream, a fantasy-derivative of the hypnotic device that had been used against him by Ann Reece? As he dressed, he considered what had seemed to happen. The Merlica incident had been most disturbing. He recalled uneasily his first feeling that it was not really his face or his body. "I wasn't in that future," he thought. "Somebody was trying to sell me on a false notion."

The reality of Merlica and of the radioactive lake and of the huge, black statue seemed suddenly less believable. Cargill grinned ruefully. When a man started to think about what the human soul might really be like, he could certainly conjure up some fanciful stuff. And yet—

And yet, he found himself reluctant to abandon entirely the idea that briefly he had broken through the illusion of material things and looked on scenes as strange as anything ever conceived by the mind of man. He remembered the old human idea that God was in everyone; and he wondered: "Viewing the lake and the statue, was I a part of God?" It hadn't quite seemed that way. He had had a purpose in creating those two life-forms, but that purpose had been there from some immensely earlier "time." It was almost as if he had been given a mission to accomplish, with *carte blanche* powers. Around the mission there was an indefinable sense of deadly urgency.

His speculations ended as a knock sounded. Cargill opened the door. Granger, the butler, stood there. He said formally: "Miss Reece wishes me to inform you that breakfast will be served in ten minutes."

Cargill entered the breakfast room, scowling with the memory of the hypnotic device that had been used against him by Ann Reece and some man. He found the girl in a filmy white dress already seated at the table. He began irritably: "You don't think that kind of hypnotism is going to work on me."

She was smugly triumphant. "It's not exactly hypnosis," she said. "The electronic tube used works on the principle I mentioned last night, where one times one etcetera equals a million or a billion, or whatever it's set for—in this case a million. When that tube was turned on last night it established a pattern in your brain that only another tube set differently could eradicate."

She shrugged. "So you're trained. You can no longer communicate in any way to anybody the knowledge you have of the plan. And when you hear the cue your legs will carry you to the pyramid power house. Your hands will throw the switch. And you'll do all this exactly at twelve o'clock noon or midnight, Shadow City time—whichever comes next—after you've been given the signal."

"Just a minute," said Cargill. He had been listening with a strained sense of unreality. Now abruptly he tried to snatch a shred of victory from the implacable fact.

"What day," he asked grimly, "will this happen?"

She was calm. "I don't think a date was set. I believe the pattern was established in your mind that would leave that flexible. Anyway, I was not given the information, the reason being that somehow you might force it out of me. You'll find out—when it happens." She broke off. "Better finish your breakfast. There'll be an air force floater here to pick you up in half an hour."

Cargill had forgotten about the air force, and he was impressed. These people seemed determined. Things were moving fast.

13

There must be something he could say or do to make sure that things happened right for himself, Cargill thought as he stood among the volor pilots later that morning. It was obvious the attack couldn't take place for at least two months. That much he knew. He had lived slightly over two months with Lela Bouvy and had listened to a Shadow City radio-TV station right up to the last.

Just for a moment, with Ann Reece, he had forgotten that. He'd never forget it again. He was living a time-paradox existence and for all he knew the paradox was even more intricate than he could hope to guess or imagine. But he'd have to make sure that there was delay. He'd have to force this situation to his will.

Warily he looked around him. The day was perfect. It was good to be alive and standing on this verdantly green hillside. The fleecy white of the small cumulus clouds that floated lazily in the higher vault of the sky only served to emphasize its blueness. An occasional breeze rustled through the leaves of the trees and puffed against his cheeks, bringing the smell of growing things. In the distance he could see the slow yellow water of a broad river. The flats that spread between him and that wide expanse of water were covered with clumps of swamp willow and a kind of coarse stiff grass whose tall serrated blades looked sharp and forbidding even at this distance.

Cargill wondered if he were looking down on the Mississippi River. The possibility excited him. He pictured himself standing here in the twenty-fourth century, looking down at the great river, its muddy, sluggish water so little changed after all these centuries.

From somewhere in the rear of the group of pilots a man said curtly, "I still don't approve of this man Cargill being here as an adviser. It's a Shadow trick of some kind."

Cargill turned stiffly and saw that the speaker was an intense-looking young man with dark brown eyes and a hawk-like nose. The officer, a full-fledged pilot, reminded him of Lauer. There was the same hard questioning tone, the same rebelliousness against the decisions of those higher in authority.

An older officer, who had been introduced to Cargill as Flight Commander Greer, said in a tone of mild reproof, "Withrow, the presence of Captain Cargill makes all our plans possible. Besides, he's here. We're committed. My own opinion is that if we learn even a little from him about air tactics and strategy of World War Two and after we'll be amply repaid in lives saved."

"And I," said Cargill, "will try to assure that I also survive the attack." It was a point he intended to keep driving home—that he had a stake now in their success.

There was no time for Withrow to comment. Dark specks appeared among the fleecy clouds. Almost instantly, the sky was full of volors. They came in over the river, low and in close formation. Even as Cargill watched the rushing machines he was aware that the group of officers were watching him. They expected a reaction. The question was, what should his response be?

He strained to recall the thousands of planes that he had seen in action, the scores of times he had stood on the battered soil of Korea and watched allied and enemy planes maneuver for the kill.

The volors whistled by a few hundred feet above the ground. He judged their speed to be as great as that of a jet plane. With a hiss of tortured air the volors plunged past. Cargill turned to follow their flight but they were already gone into the glare of the sun in the eastern sky—and the time had undoubtedly come for him to say something.

He began to ask questions. "Just what is the nature of the assault you're planning? Will you attack in flight formation or is it going to be individual ships diving down?"

Withrow said coldly, "Their protective pyramid of energy goes down and we dive in."

"We plan to attack without regard for danger," said Commander Greer.

Cargill was silent. He knew that kind of attitude, and it was basically sound except for one thing. He said, "I'd like to see this from the other side before I tell you my ideas." He pointed. "From up there. Can we go up?"

He sat presently in the co-pilot's chair in the control room and watched the volor climb. The machine rocketed upward like a shooting star. Cargill was squeezed back into his seat. The blood seemed to drain from his body. And then he felt the ship leveling off, and he saw the earth flow by below. Cargill finally turned to the men who were crowded into a series of small seats in the control room. He said to Commander Greer, "How many weapons do you have aboard?"

The officer leaned forward and indicated a trigger

device in front of the pilot. "From here," he said, "you can see everything below us. You just have to make these hair lines balance on the target, then press the trigger. The billion-tube goes into action."

Cargill nodded, unhappily. One times one times one times one times zero equalled a billion with this tube, the power of which could be varied at will. He had learned some trick mathematics at college, where one times one equalled one and a half and one plus one equalled three. But this was a million, billion, quadrillion times different. Here was the power source of this era: a variable tube. From what he had seen and heard he gathered that it provided an energy flow of a non-electric nature.

He stopped his thoughts. They had turned and were rushing back toward the city. They crossed the river like a shot from a gun. The city blurred by beneath them, then they were catapulting above a tremendous forest. A second city blinked by below, came into sight again at the volor and its companions made a U-turn in perfect formation, and then the city was lost to sight in the distant haze. The speed of the volors was colossal. Cargill had a singing feeling of wonder at their rate of travel.

Before he could speak again the capital showed ahead and they were diving. The ground rushed up to meet them. He saw the firing fields ahead. The pilot gripped the firing device and pressed the trigger gently. Flame rolled up from below, a colossal sheet of it. Cargill strained to look back through the transparent floor. He had a brief glimpse of a raging inferno, then that was gone behind them.

From the back of the control room the satirical voice of Withrow said, "Well, Captain Cargill, what advice can you offer us?"

The man sounded arrogant. His tone indicated that

he at least took it for granted that the Tweener air force was perfect as it was. Clearly he would attach no value to any minor suggestions made by a man from the remote dark ages of the twentieth century. Cargill drew a deep breath and accepted the challenge.

He said, "The fighting standards of this air force are too low. Any appreciable resistance would, in my opinion, shatter the attack. And unquestionably there will be resistance. Certain comments I have heard seem to indicate the belief that the Shadows will be over-whelmed in the first minutes of the attack. Such a notion strikes me as utterly fantastic." He did not look directly at any of the pilots individually, as he coolly went on.

He described how in his experience entire divisions had been withdrawn from battle because the men had been trained by officers who did not know how to put fighting spirit into their soldiers. "Such divisions," he explained, "can be massacred by resistance forces that would normally not even be able to slow down a fighting division."

He continued in an inexorable tone, "The shock to the nervous system of a man under fire for the first time has to be experienced to be understood. On the ground the method used was to land him on an enemy beach or otherwise commit him to battle—and then to depend on his training to carry him through. Those who survive a series of such engagements become seasoned veterans, all this providing they have been handled well by their officers. In the air force, bombers made their bomb runs and then headed for home. In this way the crews were under heavy fire for only a few minutes at a time and so those that survived became enormously cunning and skillful."

He dared to pause at that moment and take a light-ning glance at the faces of the officers. It was a long time since he had seen so many white faces. He pressed on quickly.

"As for specific suggestions for the volors, here's my picture. You've got to have weapons in the rear, so that you can fire at the target coming and going. In addition, I think you should have fighter protection for the volors that actually attack the target. And any attack should be in broken formation from all sides, unevenly and without pattern. Practice that." He broke off. "As for the pilots, let me give them lectures during the next few weeks and accustom them to the idea that they may have to endure fire for hours." He shrugged. "And now I'll have to think over any further points. Let's go down."

The landing was smooth as glass. They drew up before a huge, streamlined building. Absently, as he talked to Greer, Cargill watched Withrow walk over to a group of officers under an alcove. When he looked again a minute later the group seemed to be in earnest conversation. Presently one of the men sauntered over and Cargill recognized the officer who that morning had ferried him from Ann Reece's home to the airfield— a man named Nallen.

The man said casually, "Whenever Captain Cargill is ready, I'll take him home."

Commander Greer held out his hand. "We'll be seeing you again, Captain. Your recommendations shocked me but I can already see what you mean."

Cargill accepted the proffered handshake, but his thoughts were on Nallen and Withrow. They were obviously members of a separate group. He was determined to discover their purpose.

A few minutes later he was in a floater, heading out over the city. He had not long to wait. Withrow stepped out of the control room, followed by two other officers.

He sank into the seat across the aisle from Cargill. There was a faint ironic smile on his face.

"Captain," he said, "I have to make an apology to you. I put on an arrogant front in order to conceal my true intentions. I represent a group which is opposed to the Shadow war. It is our opinion that you cannot be violently in favor of the attack. Accordingly, we want to ask your advice and to offer you some in turn. You must try to win Miss Reece to your point of view. Grannis tells us the best method would be for you to try to make love to her—"

"Grannis!" Cargill echoed.

He sat blankly, letting the shock waves subside. But, he thought finally, with an almost owlish seriousness, that didn't make sense. Grannis was the Shadow behind these murderous schemes. Why should he advise—

He found himself stiffening. It was possible that there was no hope here. The deadly thing in all this was that if Grannis didn't like any particular development he could use his control of time to nullify it. . . . To hell with that, Cargill decided grimly. He'd fight this thing with every tool at his disposal. Here, in Withrow and his group, was possibly such a tool. He said curtly: "Just what kind of organization do you have?"

He listened thoughtfully as Withrow gave him a description of a loose-knit body of men, mostly business people and middle-aged officers, who met in each other's homes, and more or less openly discussed their opposition to the developing war. It struck Cargill finally that the very openness of it must be a protection. Evidently, the opposition was known, but was probably discounted by those in power, probably because of the very openness of the talk. It was likely, too, that the government people were so inept that they didn't recognize a rebellion when they saw it.

When Withrow had finished, Cargill said: "How many people have you got? I'd like an estimate."

"About sixty thousand."

The figure was unexpectedly large, and Cargill whistled softly to himself. He said slowly: "We'll have to change the set-up of the organization somewhat. Too many people know each other, and besides there's not enough certainty that they will act in a crisis." He described the cell system used by the Communists in the twentieth century, where only six individuals knew each other, except for the leader who had contacts with the leaders of other groups.

Cargill explained: "I hate to unload a thing like that on you, but it conquered half the world in my time, and I must admit I acquired some respect for the methods used, though I had none for the murderous ethics behind the original use of it. What makes this use of it worthwhile is that it's an attempt to stop war, not start one."

He went on, crisply: "Each cell, or group of cells, should be assigned certain projects. Estimate how many it will take, and start them to planning exactly what each group of cells, each cell group, and what each individual in the group will do when the signal is given. As I've said, back in the twentieth century, we had an opportunity to watch the forcible transfer of governmental control many, many times.

"So make a list of all the people who are likely to be troublesome, or who could be rallying points for the opposition. At a predetermined moment, you place them all under arrest, take control of the centers of communication, and start issuing orders. Get the important military leaders on our side—if you can. When there's doubt of the outcome, a leader with a large force at his disposal can sway the balance."

There were further questions from Withrow, but they

mostly involved repetition of what Cargill had already said. During the final few minutes of the flight, Cargill was silent. He thought of his dream of Merlic, the mountain city of 7301 A.D. "I'm certainly going against what they wanted," he acknowledged. "If the Tweeners have to win this war in order to make Merlica real, then by stopping the war, I'm deliberately destroying their chances."

It all seemed fantastic and far away, somehow invalidating all his thinking about the life-force. And yet, he felt doggedly convinced that his evaluation of what had "happened" in Merlic was correct. If the meeting between Bruch and himself had occurred in some weird fashion, then the plan Bruch had advanced was a trick that somebody was trying to play on him. Who the somebody might be, he had no idea; and indeed it seemed incredible when he thought of it in that way.

Who, or what, in the entire universe would be in a position to play such a trick on him? On the other hand, if it were all fantasy, then his plan to stop this oncoming Tweener-Shadow war—before he was compelled to disengage the pyramid switch—was the soundest, sanest thing he could do. The future would have to look after itself, as it had been doing for a long time now.

In spite of his doubts about the reality of what had already occurred, Cargill felt himself unwilling to give up the thoughts he had had about the possible nature of the human spirit. More than that, he had some memories from his "dream" that he wanted to consider as soon as he had a few hours to spare. What he had pictured about space-time in that dream made a curious sense indeed. The mere possibility that the material universe had existed for several million million years invalidated all ideas of the origin of life-force. By implication, all these ideas were based on a few thousand years of history. *The enormous age of the con-*

tinuum could not be ignored. It was obvious that the life-force must have come up from its far beginnings in a direct line of development.

If there were such an aliveness as the thing that men had called a soul, it was as old as the aliveness called God. And different, as a bright light is different from darkness, from the pictures of it that the minds of men had conjured in the dark, ignorant ages of human progression.

In the "dream" state, Cargill remembered tensely, he had perceived things that, when he thought of them now, pointed towards the possibility that he might be able to repeat the experience he had already had. On the basis of that memory, there were things he could do to make himself more aware. As soon as he had time, he would make another great effort.

He could not escape the feeling that further action along that line would be as vital as anything else he was doing.

Beside him, Withrow said: "Here we are."

As the machine came in for a landing, Cargill remembered about Ann Reece. "I'll woo the young lady," he said, laughing. "I don't think there will be any result, though it may distract her attention from other things."

But it was a week before he even saw her again. And then, annoyingly, she chose an evening to be home when Withrow and he had a rendezvous in the terrace garden.

14

Night. It was time for him to meet Withrow. The trouble was, it seemed to the irritated Cargill, Ann Reece showed no inclination to leave the living room. He watched her from his chair as she paced the floor. She stopped suddenly and stared at him with narrowed eyes.

"In spite of all my efforts these last few days," she said, "you've done it." Her tone was accusing. "You've put off the attack at least a month, possibly longer," she said. "I tried to convince them it was a trick on your part but Commander Greer swore that your criticism showed a grave weakness in our attack tactics. The leaders have accepted that."

She came close to him and there was no hint of the satirical lightness of manner which he had come to expect of her. "Captain Cargill," she said grimly, "you're playing this game altogether too well to suit our group. We've decided to accept the delay this time but—" She stopped. Her rather full lips were drawn into a menacing smile.

Cargill studied her, fascinated. In spite of his will to get her out of the way, the very depth of her determination caught his interest. He said slowly, "What puzzles me is that a young woman as good looking as you should be a conspirator in man's game of war."

The words were seriously spoken. Not until he had uttered them did he realize they could be an opening wedge for the lovemaking Grannis had suggested. A secondary possibility appeared. He stood up. "Where I come from," he said, "a girl had a pretty clear idea that a man in uniform who whistled at her didn't want to talk about the ideals he was fighting for."

The remark must have been unexpected, its import far from her thoughts. She gave him a startled look and then a frown creased her forehead. She said curtly, "Stay away from me."

Cargill walked slowly toward her. It seemed to him Grannis had definitely misread this cold young woman, but more sharply now he saw in her visible perturbation the solution to that secondary problem of his. "You must," he said, "have grown up under very curious circumstances. It's unusual to see a woman of your courage so afraid of herself."

She stopped backing away. Her voice showed that his words had struck deep. She said too sharply, "Our group has a single purpose, to destroy the Shadows. When that is accomplished there will be time enough to think of marrying and having children."

Cargill paused five feet from her. "I can tell you right now," he said, "you've got the wrong slant about what goes on during a war. The birth rate goes up, not down. Every hospital is filled with women carrying out some man's desperate determination to survive the war if only by proxy."

"We shall marry the survivors," said Ann Reece calmly. "It would be silly for a girl, particularly one in poor circumstances, to burden herself with a dead man's child."

Cargill said drily, "When I lecture to the volor pilots I'll be happy to tell them the girls feel a civilian is the best bet for a husband."

"I didn't say that. I said—"

Cargill cut her off. He was not going to get anywhere with this girl and therefore the sooner he put her to flight the better. "And what," he asked, "about the man to whom you've so casually assigned the job of disengaging the pyramid switch in the heart of Shadow City? Do you mean to tell me he's not even going to get a kiss from a pretty girl?"

He stepped forward and tried to take her in his arms. She evaded him and retreated to the door. Laughing, careful not to move so fast that he would actually catch her, Cargill followed. For one moment Ann Reece hesitated and then, her face scarlet with anger, she fled precipitantly along the corridor and up the broad stairs. He heard the door of her bedroom suite slam shut.

His amusement faded quickly. Cool and intent, Cargill hurried across to the French windows and out into the darkness. A minute later he was talking to Withrow, learning what he had half-expected—that it would require at least a month to set up the underground organization on the cell basis. The first week had shown the general speed of development that could be expected. Cargill's final comment was, "The important thing is that if anything goes wrong, individuals may suffer, but the organization itself will remain intact."

They separated on that note.

Later, on his way to his bedroom, he paused on impulse and knocked on Ann Reece's door. "May I come in?" he called.

There was silence and then an outraged answer. "Don't you dare even try the door."

Cargill twisted the knob noisily. The door was locked. He went on, smiling to himself, feeling quite without shame or guilt. He believed firmly with ninety percent of all the soldiers he had ever met that during war time every woman was a possible conquest—and how else could you find out her attitude unless you pursued her?

Having started to pursue Ann Reece, he intended to continue. Though after he reached his room his thoughts drifted elsewhere. He lay in bed recalling the time he had been wounded in Korea and had experienced that sense of *far awayness*. "I've got to get the exact feeling," he thought.

Presently it came to him. Moment after moment, he went through the experience, first moving through it chronologically, then in reverse. Each time he sought to pinpoint the moment when the shift from life to almost death had taken place. He noticed within himself a rising sense of excitement, an expectancy, a developing conviction that something was about to happen.

Abruptly, there was an electrifying sensation all over his body. In the distance, he saw a golden ball spinning in space. It was so beautiful, he tried to close his eyes and look away. He couldn't. It was beauty incarnate.

As he watched, he noticed that the ball emitted sparks as it spun. The sparks rushed off into space and took on spiral shapes. Now he noticed that the golden ball was made up of countless similar shapes which were part of itself.

"Why," he thought wonderingly, "it contains the entire physical universe. It *is* the universe."

Something black swirled between him and the golden thing, hiding it, blotting it out. And he knew who the enemy was—blackness, nothingness.

He felt an abrupt, unreasoning terror, a deadly panic. There was a blank, terrible urgency about the battle that was going on out there—*here*.

The life-phase of the struggle was almost lost. Everyone connected with the gigantic conflict would go down in the disaster. Much had been expected from life-force, but it was turning out to be suppressive, unthinking—not creative. So low had the spirit sunk that even death did not bring awareness of identity. For long now, this same spirit had been caught in stereotyped life-traps; it no longer even suspected defeat. As things stood, any new major disaster could bring about final destruction. . . .

Cargill grew slowly conscious of returning from a fantastic experience. He looked around the bedroom in Ann Reece's residence and wondered how wild a man's thoughts could become. "I'm going to have to stop this," he thought shakily. "A few more nightmares like that, and I'll begin to believe that the fate of the universe depends on this Tweener-Shadow fight."

He was certainly getting results of a sort—he had to admit that. Whatever these strange dreams meant, they *were* phenomena; and, what was more important, he could apparently produce the weird manifestations at will. Two successes out of two attempts was not conclusive, but he had thought things, or rather, *known* things during the experiences that suggested entirely untouched trails of perception.

There were thoughts about how space was drawn out of matter; thoughts about creation and destruction; orderly methods for tearing away the illusion that was the material universe; thoughts about the type of energy flows that had dealt with illusion and beauty. . . .

Beauty? Cargill remembered the glorious golden ball, and tensed. At the time, it had seemed the ultimate life-beginning, but it wasn't. He felt completely convinced of that, because beauty focused. Beauty was the light that kept the moth of life fluttering hopefully. It drew all attention, was the final goal of all endeavor. The far gleam of the beautiful kept a man straining all his life; and when somehow everything he grasped to him did not hold the radiance he had seen, he grew sad and sickly; and presently one of two things happened: The sadness either transformed into the apathy of death, or into the ecstatic apathy of another far-seen gleam of beauty—life after death.

Beauty would be but one aspect of Prime Thought. Prime Thought would be but one aspect of—what?

Cargill slept restlessly. He kept wakening with the memory of a golden ball so beautiful that twice he caught himself sobbing with excitement. Deliberately, he told himself to stop being a fool. After all, he'd need all the sleep he could get. It seemed to him finally that he had barely closed his eyes when Granger knocked on the door with the advice that: "Commander Greer called, sir, and a ship will be here to pick you up in an hour."

There was no sign of Ann at breakfast, which reminded him that he had decided to pursue her. The trouble was that she evidently avoided him. During the days that followed he caught only fleeting glimpses of her. As he entered a room, she left it. Several times, she was leaving the house just as he was returning from a weary day. Every night, without fail, he tried her door. It was always locked, and only occasionally could he be sure that she was inside.

A month went by. And still the secret organization was not of satisfactory size. The trouble, according to Withrow, was that men known to be opposed to the war adjusted slowly to the concept that a government could be seized from within. It was apparently a brand new idea in this remote age.

For six weeks the air force kept Cargill busy. He was flown to distant stations to give his lectures and was able to form his first estimate of the size of the Tweenerland—the Tweeners called it America. This presumption, considering their small numbers, did much to indicate their lack of perspective.

The new civilization was bounded on the west by the foothills of the Rockies, on the north by what Cargill guessed to be about the southern border of Montana, in the east by a line curving southwest from the lower tip of Lake Michigan, and in the south by northern Texas. Although it was a tremendous area for three million people to control, there was no doubt of this control.

Cargill could imagine that eventually they would extend their domination over the entire continent. He learned that far-sighted Tweeners were already filing claims to vast acreage. He remembered the landless millions of the twentieth century, and it struck him that already the errors of the past were being repeated. "If I get out of this business alive," he told himself, "I'll try to put a stop to that."

Wherever he looked he saw things he was better able to evaluate because of having witnessed end-results in his own age. A score of times he mentally filed away the notation, "I'll have to do something about that—later."

With each day that passed he convinced himself more completely that with his automatic knowledge he could be of enormous value to the people of this advanced age. It stiffened his will power. He walked straighter and with a firmer stride. He felt an alertness within himself, a will to action that also had behind it an enormous instinctive caution. He used words as if they were tools, perpetually aware of the possible danger that might at any moment confront him.

This caution was proved sound one evening when he entered Ann Reece's house. He was walking along the carpeted hallway toward the living room, when he heard a man's emotional voice say, "I intend to kill you both the moment he comes."

Cargill stopped as Ann shakily replied, "You're mad. You'll hang for this."

"Shut up!" The voice was intense. "I know you. You started all this. You're the one that's associated with the Shadow, Grannis. I heard all about how he came to you a year ago and you've been his echo ever since."

"I did not start it." Her answer was in a firmer tone. "The volors were already built, the plans made, when Grannis got in touch with me. I reported it to the government and I've been the contact with him ever since."

"That's what I said." The man sounded tremendously satisfied. "You're the contact. With you and this new fellow dead, that'll stop the whole rotten business."

Cargill heard no more. He was racing back toward the front door. He guessed that the would-be assassin had come in through the garden and was probably facing into the living room, watching the other entrances. Cargill slipped out of the door, went around the house, through the gate and—stealthily now, though still swiftly—moved across the terrace. One of the French windows was open. He crept up beside it, partly sheltered by the wooden frames. There he paused to determine the situation inside.

The intruder was saying in a high-pitched tone, "My folks were Planiacs. They took the Shadow training and failed. But they came here and I was born into a good home. I had civilized upbringing, a decent education. I married a wonderful girl and I've got two fine kids. The Shadows made that possible." His voice lifted even higher. "You and those murderous scoundrels who planned the attack hate the Shadows because you all failed. Now you're trying to force the rest of us to your rotten notions. You want to destroy what you aren't smart enough to win."

Cargill saw the man, a powerful-looking individual. His back was to the terrace, and a spitter was barely visible in his fingers. It pointed in the general direction of the girl.

Ann Reece said scathingly, "You ought to be ashamed of yourself, a big man like you acting like a cowardly child. Have you thought of what's going to happen to your wife and children if you do anything foolish now?" Her voice was calm and forceful. She sounded as if she had got all her courage back. She said, "I'm going to give you one chance. Leave now and I won't report this. Quick, make up your mind."

"I'll show you what mind I'm going to make up," the man said violently. He waved the spitter menacingly. "In just about one second—"

He must have heard a sound or noticed a change of expression on Ann Reece's face for he started to turn. In that unbalanced position he was caught by Cargill's tackle. The big man went down heavily but firmly. Swiftly, brutally, Cargill plunged on top of him, aware that Ann Reece had snatched the spitter.

"Get away from him," she yelled at Cargill. "I'll spit him."

The stranger was also yelling. "Help!" he called. "Manot! Gregory!"

There was a sound. "All right," said a cold voice from the door. "Ann, put down that gun. Cargill, get up."

Cargill hesitated and then, tense with the new danger, climbed to his feet. He was puzzled. The situation somehow seemed wrong. He turned slowly and saw the two men in the uniforms of volor pilots. The man who had spoken returned his gaze steadily.

"Just testing, Captain, just testing," he said. "We've had reports about some kind of underground scheme and so we decided to try to get a reaction."

Even as the man spoke, Cargill's mind darted over the events but found nothing out of the way. Ann had

acted in character—why not? It was her character—
and he himself had done only what could have been
expected. He said slowly, "I hope you learned what you
wanted."

The pilot said with apparent frankness, "Exactly
what we wanted." He bowed to Ann Reece, who was
unusually pale. "I want to congratulate you, Miss
Reece, on your courage. And don't blame us. Grannis
suggested this test."

To the big man, who was just getting up from the
floor, he said curtly, "You put on a good act. But now
come along."

When they had gone Cargill walked over to the
young woman and said, "That was very unkind of them.
Here, you'd better sit down. They don't seem to realize
what a shock a thing like this can be to the system."

He was thinking, "Grannis again—what could the
Shadow be up to?"

Ann Reece allowed herself to be led to a chair. She
looked up at him, her face still very white. She said in
a low voice, "Thank you for saving my life, Captain."

"I didn't actually save it," said Cargill. "After all, it
was a fake menace."

She said stiffly, "You didn't know that when you
made the attack. I don't know how I can ever repay
you."

"Forget it. I thought I was saving my own as well."

She seemed not to hear. "They were testing me," she
said. "Me!" She seemed overwhelmed.

Cargill started to say something but stopped himself.
For the first time he realized that this girl was under-
going a profound emotional experience. He watched
her sharply for a few moments, then reached down and
took her hand. "I think you'd better go to your room
and lie down," he said.

She let him lead her. At the door of her bedroom,

she stopped. A touch of color came into her cheeks. She didn't look at him. "Captain," she said, "tonight I realized what you meant about war being different from any idea that I had of it. And I'm sorry for my share in bringing you into this desperate danger. Can you ever forgive me?"

Cargill thought of the imminent rebellion and said coolly, "I'm in. I've accepted the idea. I'll fight with everything I've got to make sure that I survive." He added, "You'd better lie down."

He opened the door for her. She stepped through and there was more color in her face as she gave him a quick glance. She said breathlessly, "Captain, you said something once about a reward for a soldier . . . To-night, when you try the knob of this door, you'll find that it . . . turns."

She slipped all the way in. The door closed gently. The faint perfume of her presence lingered. Cargill walked slowly on to his own room. He was more touched than he cared to admit. The only annoyance was, when he tried the door an hour later it was locked.

Cargill stood with one hand on the knob, baffled, a little irritated, not quite ready to give up. Most of the girls he had gone after in his career did not fall easily into a man's arms. Affinity had to be established; and apparently in Ann's case, the rescue hadn't been enough. He was still standing, undecided, when he heard a sound inside. The next instant the door opened, and the girl's strangely pale face peered through a crack about three inches wide. Cargill could see that she wore a blue negligee with not much else on underneath.

She whispered, "I just can't go through with what I said. I'm sorry."

Cargill sighed as many a man had before him in a similar situation. But now that he had a conversation started, he was not prepared to let go. "May I come in and talk to you? I swear you don't have to be afraid of me."

She hesitated, and he seized the opportunity to push gently at the door. At that, she yielded, and retreating into the bedroom, turned on a bedside light, and crept into the bed. Protectively, she drew a soft pink quilt about her. It failed to hide the tanned skin that was visible through her negligee above the waist. Cargill took one of the pillows, placed it against the headboard. Seating himself on the bed, he relaxed back against the pillow.

"How old are you, Ann?" he asked gently.

"Twenty-four." She looked at him questioningly.

"If you hadn't backed out of this promise tonight," Cargill asked frankly, "would I have been your first lover?"

She hesitated, then shrugged. Something of her blasé manner came back. She laughed curtly. "No, I tried sex once when I was seventeen. Something must have been wrong because all I can remember is pain, pain, pain. I've got to admit that scared me." She laughed again, tensely. "I've heard good reports about it since then."

"Where I come from," said Cargill, "seventy per cent of women are frigid because their husbands never learned the first simple principles of lovemaking. They're not really frigid, you understand, as many a soldier can tell you about many a so-called frigid wife of another man." He broke off. "Is it that seventeen year old memory that holds you back now?"

She was silent. "I did think of it." she admitted. She began to laugh suddenly, hysterically. "My dear," she said, when she could control herself, "I'm sure this is really the funniest conversation I've had in a long time. Come on over here before I trap myself with words. I'm very skillful at talking myself into emotional corners."

From that moment, Ann Reece was his girl.

15

She didn't realize how completely she was his at first. She had no idea how much emotion went along with a physical commitment. If she had been experienced it might have been different. She might have been able to divide herself, figuratively, into two individuals, on the one hand the patriot, on the other the mistress of the prisoner.

The patriot, in spite of the rude shock of the test, remained fairly intact for five days. At that point she had her first breakdown. Thereafter, she cried easily in Cargill's presence. On the eighth day she came out openly with the suggestion that they find some method of escape. Her plans were vague, curiously impractical for someone who had been so hard-headed. She had a fine contempt for Cargill's objections. Half a dozen times within the space of a few days she lost her temper with him.

She put a pressure on him which added to his own anxiety. On the twelfth day he visited the airport and angrily drew Withrow aside. "I have a feeling," he said, "that your group is stalling. There's a weakness here somewhere, an unwillingness to burn your bridges."

Withrow looked unhappy. "There's something to that," he admitted. "All I hear is excuses."

Cargill could understand that. Thinking of these leaders who had never before seen action, he was reminded of the eve of battle. As one stormy dawn broke he had thought and hoped that surely the attack would be called off. And, curiously, he had thought simultaneously, "Thank heaven, the issue is being forced at last."

This issue also had to be forced. And there was only one man who had the motivation, the will and the experience to force it. He said in measured tone, "Withrow, the attack must be made not later than tomorrow morning. If it isn't made I will inform Commander Greer who the ringleaders are."

Withrow turned pale. "You wouldn't dare."

Cargill said quietly, "Perhaps you'd better let the others think that I would dare."

He returned the pilot's gaze steadily. At last Withrow sighed. He held out his hand. "You've named the day," he said. "Thank you."

They shook hands silently and separated.

Cargill had his first premonition of disaster as he entered the house shortly after dark. Ann, her face gray, met him at the door. "They've posted guards around the house," she whispered. "They're sending you to Shadow City tonight."

Cargill stood stock still, dimly aware of her fluttering hands stroking his arm.

She whispered, "I'm sorry."

He patted her hand absently. He was thinking, "Is this timed? Do they know or suspect?" Aloud he said, "Why did they select tonight?"

"Grannis—" she began.

That shocked him. With an astounded fury he cut

her off, gripped her shoulders cruelly. "But I thought you were his contact!"

"I used to be," she said miserably. "I don't know what's happened. Please, you're hurting me."

He let her go with a mumbled apology. His sense of imminent catastrophe was greater. The incredible, fantastic, mysterious Grannis had taken one more step in his inexplicable scheme. But this time he had moved in a direct and deadly fashion. Whatever else Grannis had in mind it was clear that he intended Captain Morton Cargill to experience the terrible risk of going to Shadow City.

Finally, he patted her gently and stroked her hands. He could feel her trembling. He stepped away from her and said: "Has any date been set?"

She shook her head. "I'm out of this picture. They're telling me nothing."

He said softly, "Go and see about dinner, Ann. I'll investigate the situation."

He headed for the terrace, crossed the garden in the dark, climbed over the fence—he was stopped by a guard.

"Get back!" The command was curtly spoken. A spitter glinted in the man's hand.

Cargill obeyed readily and headed immediately for the gate that led to the front of the house. It was unlocked. But as he stepped through, a soldier came from behind a tree and angrily motioned him to return.

Altogether in the course of a few minutes he counted nine guards, all armed, all aware of his identity. When he re-entered the house Commander Greer was there with Ann.

"Sorry, Captain," he said, "but we just couldn't take any chances. Grannis advised us that there was going to be a rebellion and so we've ordered all officers to report to their units. Just in case there is a disturbance you leave right after dinner for Shadow City."

Greer remained for dinner. When the meal was over, as Cargill and Ann followed the officer to the outer hall, she whispered, "Find some way of kissing me good-by. I'll pretend to resist."

A volor-powered floaterlike craft waited for them on the lawn. Cargill turned to Ann and, mustering all his sardonicism, said, "Miss Reece, once it amused you to say that you would kiss me good-by when I left like this. I demand that kiss."

He didn't wait for assent. Firmly he stepped to her, put his finger under her chin, lifted her head and bent his own. The kiss he gave her was outrageously bold, and the only trouble was that she didn't resist very hard. Fortunately, the guards thought his move an attack and pulled him away from her.

"Good-by, darling," said Cargill cheerfully. "I'll be back."

He was surprised to realize that he meant it. He was tremendously drawn to Ann Reece. "I thought I loved them all," he told himself in almost drunken confusion. "Lela and—" He remembered some of the wonderfully personable girls who had been milestones in his life up until 1954—but Ann was different.

"Well, I'll be damned," he thought. "I've fallen for the girl."

The metal door clanged shut behind him. The ship lifted violently. As he sank into a seat the black reality of his position crushed down upon his spirits.

He braced himself finally and thought: "I've still got to decide what I'm going to do."

Hopefully, he looked at the crew that was taking him to his destination. He recognized none of the five volor-men aboard, but they must have been among those to whom he had lectured. Although he doubted that he could subvert them, he thought there was no harm in trying.

He waited till the co-pilot looked back from the cockpit, and then he beckoned him. The man spoke to his commander, apparently received permission, and came striding back.

"Captain?" he said politely.

For some reason the remark struck Cargill as excruciatingly funny. He began to laugh. "Captain!" he repeated aloud, and the word again set him into a gale of laughter.

Tears streaming down his eyes, Cargill looked up at the other. "Lieutenant—" he began. He stopped. *"Lieutenant!"* "Lieutenant" was even funnier than "Captain." After a time, he controlled the new, greater burst of laughter and managed to say: "Lieutenant, have you made your will?"

"No, sir." The man was stiff.

Cargill laughed that one off, resigned now—to his hysteria; he'd seen men in this state before. The best way to handle it was to give it full release. "Better make your will, Lieutenant. Men die in war, you know. Or are you a behind-the-lines man?"

"No, sir, I volunteered."

"Volunteered!" roared Cargill, and this time he laughed for minutes. He said finally, between gasps: "That's the spirit, boy. What we need in this army are volunteers, ready to die for dear old Alma Mater— pardon me, I'm getting my places mixed up, or is it my spaces?"

That was a special joke, out of his wild dreams; and he nearly cracked a rib before that laughter subsided.

"You've got to face reality, sir," said the co-pilot, evidently a serious young man.

It was almost too much. When he finally stopped laughing, Cargill said, "Young man, keep right on facing reality, and be sure to keep an eye on the facts, and report to me every day. That's the important thing. Keep in touch."

"I'm sorry that you're taking this so hard," said the young man.

"It's not the initial cost," roared Cargill. "It's the upkeep. Young love cannot live on bread and cheese alone, you know. They also need a Cadillac—pardon me, a floater. *Pardon me!*" His attention was momentarily caught by the phrase. Several times he fumbled it with his tongue, savoring the thousands of times he had used it. "Be sure to pardon me," he said at last, soberly. "Yes, sir, I've got to be pardoned."

He saw that he had lost his audience. The co-pilot was heading forward. Cargill stared after him with an almost owlish concern. He said aloud to no one in particular: "He's going to report that I'm off my rocker."

An older man in a captain's uniform came back and bent over him. "We've got an all-night trip ahead of us, Captain Cargill," he said.

Cargill nodded thoughtfully. "Would you suggest that I try to sleep, sir?" he asked gravely.

"I would most certainly suggest it," was the firm reply.

"Get my forty winks, would you say, sir?" Cargill asked.

There was a pause; then quietly: "Perhaps you would like a sedative, Captain."

Cargill sighed. The laughter seemed to be exhausted. His heart was no longer in the project. And it seemed that he had learned something: These men were serious. At the assigned hour, they would make their volor dives on the Shadow City, prepared to face the grave risk of personal destruction. Cargill sighed again. "I'll go quietly, Captain," he said.

When the officer departed, Cargill sat for many minutes staring out into the gathering darkness. "I needed that," he thought. "I've been holding too many strings: trying to be a puppetmaster when actually I'm only a puppet." He thought of all the strings he had laid out for himself, each one attached to an iron that he had put into some remote fire. Looking back, it all seemed pretty futile. Looking ahead . . .

Whose side was he on, really? Which cause *should* he support? If the Tweeners won—and he was not killed—he could go back to Ann. Never again would he have to fear being returned to the therapy room of the Shadows. It was something to think about, not at all to be despised. Lan Bruch of unborn Merlica, city out of a dream, would likewise approve.

So what, if it hadn't been Morton Cargill up there in that future. How could he expect it to be? By 7301 A.D., the bones of Captain Cargill would have had four thousand years of mouldering.

"Why resist the inevitable?" Cargill asked.

He thought presently of at least one reason. The Tweeners were starting this war. That was one hundred per cent against them in his book. If it were left to the Shadows, there would be no war. That was one hundred per cent in their favor.

It was hard, it seemed to Cargill, to argue against a two hundred per cent differential in favor of the Shadows.

He slept. He awakened to a sunlit world. A member of the crew, holding a tray, was bending over him. "Got breakfast for you, sir. Captain says for you to eat and then come forward."

It was the coffee, particularly, that Cargill enjoyed. He entered the control room, his cup still in his hand. He was prepared to be friendly in exchange for more coffee.

"You can see Shadow City," said the pilot, "if you look straight ahead through the mist." He broke off. "Ed, give Captain Cargill your seat."

The co-pilot promptly rose. Cargill settled into the seat and looked out. Fog and haze blurred the horizon ahead. Mountain peaks seemed to waver in the uncertain light. It was hard to distinguish one shape from another.

Suddenly, he saw the pyramid. It was uneven to his vision and very small, as the peak of a stupendous mountain seems toylike from afar. He estimated that it must be at least a hundred miles ahead.

The floater continued to move toward it at normal floater speed. This was natural enough—Cargill had gathered that they didn't want the Shadows to suspect anything unusual about this particular machine.

Half an hour went by and all that time the fantastic city ahead grew larger. The towering pyramid shape came into sharper and sharper focus. At ten miles, it was a tremendously high pointed structure, set on a vast base. It straddled a nest of mountains. From five miles away the pyramid resembled a slope of glass through which Cargill could see the buildings concentrated in the central area. Seen close-up, the pyramid seemed anything but a powerful energy screen. It was even harder to grasp that he was here to disconnect the energy of that screen so that the Tweeners could dive down in their marvelous volors upon the unprotected metal and concrete of Shadow City—shadow no more.

"We land below there at the terminal." The pilot pointed at a building that stood at the edge of a forest.

No other words were spoken. The floater came gently down on the green sward a hundred and fifty feet from a long low building. Cargill stepped out without being asked. The door clicked shut behind him. He watched as the machine rose into the sky and headed off toward the east.

Cargill turned and automatically started toward the terminal. And then he stopped. "I'm free," he thought. "They didn't wait to make sure that I would go in. Why shouldn't I just head downhill and lose myself in the wilderness?"

The surroundings appeared immeasurably desolate: peaks, crags, valleys, ravines and everywhere the primitive forest. It would probably take several days to reach the foothills. But it was a way out. Cargill made as if to turn. Nothing happened. He stood very still, startled. He remembered the tube that had "trained" him. Carefully he walked forward, then abruptly tried to twist on his heels. The muscles wouldn't respond. Pale but determined he thought, "I'll just stay here. I'll act so queerly that the Shadows will become suspicious."

His legs began to move, easily, naturally, without any sense of strain. He tried to stop them, but he had apparently forgotten how. Involuntarily, but without any of the appearance or feeling of being an automaton, he walked across the lawn toward the terminal building. He was able to pause at the door, but only long enough to peer briefly through the thick glass into a marble alcove. A young woman inside smiled at him and pressed a button. The door opened.

A moment later Cargill was inside.

16

Cargill paused again just inside the door. In spite of his tenseness, he was curious. He stared with interest and some excitement at the young woman behind the alcove desk. A Shadow? he wondered. She had something of the intelligent look that he'd half expected. But there was also an intensity about her that was hard to define.

The young receptionist smiled and said in a rich, friendly voice, "We're so very glad to see you here of your own free will. We welcome you with all our hearts. We wish you luck. We want you to be one of us."

Cargill studied her warily. He recognized an emotional appeal when he heard one and he was impressed by the psychology of it. However, he was not so prepared to accept it as applied to himself. He had too many walls erected against chance breakthroughs of an emotional nature.

The young woman was speaking again. "You go through this door," she said as she pressed a button.

Cargill had already glanced through the door. It was wonderfully transparent and led into a marble-walled corridor that slanted off to the right. He smiled at the receptionist, said, "Thank you!" and walked through the door she had opened for him. Two nice-looking older women—Cargill guessed about forty years each—sat at a records section to the right.

One of them said, "You're a fine-looking young man. We wish you luck."

The other came out from behind the counter. "Come with me."

She led the way along a corridor that was lined with glass-fronted cubbyholes. They reminded Cargill of the way some department stores arranged their credit sections. In each office was a desk and two chairs. Cargill's guide paused at one of the entrances. "Here's your prize of the day, Moira." She touched Cargill's arm lightly. "Good luck, young man."

"Thank you."

He spoke automatically, then walked into the office. The young woman looked up and surveyed him thoughtfully for a moment. Then she said, "I like you."

"Thanks," said Cargill somewhat drily. It seemed to him he was beginning to get the idea. And it was pretty impressive. In little more than a minute they had tried to make him welcome. He saw that Moira was studying him understandingly.

"You're cynical?" she said.

That was unexpected. Cargill protested, "I think you've got an excellent system."

"It didn't hurt me to say I like you," said the girl, "so I said it. Do you mind closing the door?"

Cargill closed it and remarked, "It's a very good technique for making new arrivals feel at home."

She shook her head. "I'm very happy to disillusion you. That's the way we live. Part of our life is so tremendously intellectual, so precise and scientific, that we long ago adopted a warmly emotional personal approach on every level of our community life. You'll see when you get into the city. But now, please sit down."

As Cargill complied, she took out a card and picked up a pen. "You're Morton Cargill, aren't you?"

Cargill stiffened. He had had a false name quivering on the tip of his tongue. Now he sank a little lower in his chair, silent and alarmed. It seemed to him that he had no recourse but to admit the truth. The chilling effect of the identification grew. He had a sense of being finally committed. Everything he had done since coming to the twenty-fourth century had been done under pressure. And yet, throughout, he'd had the feeling that he would be able to control his destiny. That feeling was gone. In spite of all his actions and counteractions here he was just where the plotters wanted him to be.

He braced himself to the reality. His opposition, it seemed to him, must now be narrowed down to one individual. If he could somehow kill Grannis, that act, and that alone, might still sway the balance. Aloud he said, "Am I expected?"

She nodded but said nothing. He watched as she wrote down his name, his nervousness growing. He thought of more implications of the recognition. Mentally, he pictured himself back in the original therapy room, being killed while Betty Lane, who had made the original complaint against him, looked on. The recollection put a pressure on him. He had to have more information. "I don't understand how you could possibly know my name. Do you know in advance the name of everyone who comes here?"

"Oh, no. You're special." She looked up. "You've come for the training, of course?"

It was only partly a question. The point was one which she evidently wanted to be taken for granted. Cargill decided temporarily to abandon his effort to find out how these people had learned his name. The young woman smiled at him again. Suddenly she looked so young that he said with impulsive curiosity: "Are you a Shadow?"

The girl nodded. "Yes, I am."

"You don't always maintain the Shadow shape then?"

"Whatever for?" She sounded astonished. "That's a highly specialized state of being." As if she suspected his instant fascination with the subject matter, she said hurriedly, "Have you any idea what your responsibilities will be when you become a Shadow?"

Cargill noted that she said "when" and not "if." It gave him a heady sensation and emboldened him to ask directly, "How did you know my name?"

"Time paradox."

"You mean something has *already* happened that you know about but I don't?"

She nodded.

"What?" asked Cargill with automatic absorption.

She shrugged. "It's really very simple. For your own private reasons you've been doing things for months. We don't know why but it brought you to our attention."

Cargill was cautious. "No one has investigated my reasons?"

The woman smiled. "Naturally not. But now—it's customary for me to explain what our work is."

Cargill restrained the questions that quivered on his lips. He forced himself to sit back. He watched the woman intently as she spoke.

"We Shadows," she began, "are trying to undo the effects of the psychological disaster that demoralized the human race, beginning in the twentieth century. The pressure of civilization was apparently too much for millions of people. Everywhere men sought escape and they found the means late in 1980 in the newly invented floaters. When it became apparent that a mass flight from civilization was under way psychologists searched frantically for the causes. Naturally, in accordance with their training, they looked into the immediate past of each individual and so it was only gradually that they learned the truth.

"It turned out to be a combination of inherited weakness and justified withdrawal from intolerable pressures. But man can build any civilization he desires. So the problem was to free him by nullifying the experiences and disasters that had befallen the affected protoplasmic lines, sometimes one, sometimes many generations earlier. Jung, one of the pioneer analysts, suspected its existence very early. He called it the ancestral shadow. After many years of experiment, a technique was developed for reaching into the past and rectifying to some extent the effects of the original disaster.

"The results are becoming more apparent to us every year. Planiacs are accepting our training in ever-increasing numbers. Unfortunately, since they start from such a low level of culture, most of them fail in their purpose. The result of the test, I must explain, is something we cannot control. It is purely mechanical. The individual either responds to the training and becomes a Shadow or does not respond and so gains only the educational benefits that enable him to become a Tweener. But the Shadow shape depends on a balance within the individual. We know how that balance functions but we have no artificial method for producing it. Do you understand that?"

Cargill said, genuinely interested, "What types of people generally succeed?"

"Your type," said Moira. She stood up. She pointed at a closed door to his right, which till that instant he hadn't noticed. "You go through there. Good luck."

Cargill stood up uncertainly but he opened the door. There was a grassy lawn outside and a spread of flowering shrubs that hid his view. He stepped across the threshold, walked around the shrubbery and saw with a start that he was inside Shadow City.

With a hissing intake of his breath Cargill stopped. He was on a plateau, looking down at the city proper. But how had he come here so quickly? It was a mile at least to the terminal center where he had reported.

In spite of his previous knowledge of their method of transportation he felt compelled to turn around and investigate. When he looked he saw that there was a shallow cliff behind him. It was about fifty feet high and it was covered with growth. Flowers of every hue peered from among shining green leaves, and the dry cool air was heavy with the blended perfume.

For a moment, Cargill stood there, breathing deeply in relaxed enjoyment, and then he saw the door. It was in the side of the cliff. He went to it and it seemed ordinary enough. On impulse he turned the knob, pushed and stepped through. He was back in terminal center.

The woman was still at her desk. "Curious?" she asked.

Cargill said intently, "How does it work?"

She pointed up at the top of the door frame. "There's a tube up there. It focuses on you as you step over the threshold."

"Is it instantaneous?"

She shook her head. "Not exactly."

Cargill hesitated. Another thought had struck him. There had been no resistance to his returning here. The "training" Ann Reece had given him had, earlier, prevented him from so much as turning around, but now he had come back a mile and a half.

"If I could tell this woman about Grannis," he thought tensely.

He parted his lips, swallowed, tried again but no

words came. He guessed the explanation. His return this time had been natural, had had nothing to do with opposition to the "training." The moment, however, that he had consciously tried to take advantage of the situation the pressure resumed. He found himself struggling against the inhibition as he stood there. It was a silent fight but desperate for all that. He could think the words. He could even imagine the exact shape his mouth should take to utter them. But they didn't come. He swallowed again and gave it up. He said quietly, "I guess I'd better be going."

He stepped through the door and found himself once more in the park. A minute later he was walking along a pathway when he heard the sweet sound of a child's laughter. A woman said something in a pleasant voice. Presently mother and daughter—Cargill assumed the relationship—emerged from behind a large path. Cargill watched them till they moved out of sight behind a line of brush. He tried to envision this city, its protective screen gone, attacked by swarms of volors. It was a deadly scene he saw and it stiffened him.

"The Tweeners are just a bunch of murderers," he thought grimly, "so long as they intend to carry through with that plan. I'll wreck that notion if it's the last thing I ever do."

From where he stood on the hillside, he could see a park with dozens of floaters standing in neat rows. There seemed to be no one around. Cargill headed down and came presently to the entrance of the park. A small signboard there stated:

NEWCOMERS
Use These Floaters
GO TO
Square Building
AT CENTER OF CITY

Cargill climbed into one of the machines, guided it up and in the indicated direction. He had no difficulty finding the square building. It was surrounded by a series of round structures, and on its roof was a huge sign that spelled out: TRAINING CENTER. Another smaller sign said:

Land on Roof.

Once out of the floater Cargill followed a line of arrows to a doorway, down a flight of marble stairs and into a marble corridor. Both sides of the hall were lined with transparent plexiglass doors. At a great desk behind a counter to his left sat a woman. Stepping over to her, Cargill identified himself a little nervously and waited while she consulted a folder.

"You will receive your first training," she said pleasantly, "in cubicle eleven. It's down the corridor to your right." She smiled at him. "Good luck."

His heels clacked on the marble floor as he walked, giving him an assured feeling of being in friendly surroundings. Coming to Shadow City had burdened his mind with the fear that he would find only the alien and the unknown. But the human beings he had met so far were the friendliest and most relaxed he had ever seen. That made him uneasy for it didn't fit at all with the ruthless *therapy* they had planned for him. And yet the little girl he had seen in the park was so childlike, so normal. He could feel the pressure of this gathering crisis closing in upon him. What was he to do?

The thought ended as he came to cubicle eleven. He hesitated, opened the door and stepped inside.

17

Although similar in construction to the cubicle in which he had been interviewed at terminal center, this one was larger. He saw a desk, one chair (not two), and another door—he wondered if it led to some remote point. There was also a mirror on the wall to his left. Desiring to know his surroundings, he tried the door. It was locked. As he turned back a voice spoke out of the air in front of him.

"Sit down, please."

Although the tone was friendly, Cargill felt the tension rise in him. Not knowing what to expect, Cargill seated himself.

The voice spoke again. "See this!"

The room flashed into pitch darkness and in the air only about two feet in front of Cargill's eyes appeared a stream of radiant energy. It was a delicate lacework of brightness and looked like a filament out of its vacuum environment.

The voice said, "You are witnessing electron flow in a vacuum tube. Now watch."

The direction of the flow began to change. It followed a more winding path and seemed to be turning on some kind of an axis. Several moments passed before he saw that the flow direction was a distinct spiral.

The voice said, "Old in mathematics is the idea that two forces exerted at right angles to each other produce a diagonal curve of motion. And so one times one may equal one and one-half or some fraction thereof, something other than it might equal in the old classical mathematics. Watch as we bring the spirals closer together."

To Cargill they had seemed close as they were. But now as he stared at the filament, the spiraling line of light seemed to draw together, a tiny bit only. "One times one times one times one times zero," said the voice, "equals a million."

Again there was a change in the flow. The filaments were closer together.

". . . equal a billion," said the voice. There was a pause. The filament glowed on. Then the voice said, "Now, we superimpose ordinary infra-red light powered by a tiny battery. And we have—a spitgun."

The outline of a spitgun appeared in the air and Cargill saw how the tube was fastened into it, how the battery powered it.

"We superimpose," said the voice, "a magnetic field. Now we can bend steel."

Cargill saw how that was done.

The voice went on, "We superimpose ordinary sunlight—and we have a sun-motor, power source of the floater. A score of energy possibilities suggest themselves."

In quick succession, three of these possibilities were shown: how the volor worked, a method of turning a wheel, and the way thoughts were imposed on a brain.

"Now," said the voice, "would you like to do these various things with your own mind? We focus a millionpower brain-pattern tube on the somaesthenic centers of the parietal lobe of the left hemisphere of the brain—since you are right handed—and establish a high conditionality of flow patterned exactly after that of the steptube itself. We thus create a nerve tube in the brain. Since it is not possible for you in your normal body to superimpose other rhythms on the flow of this organic tube, we use the new control to alter slightly the atomic pattern of the body. And so, by drawing on the broadcast power of the pyramid screen, we create the Shadow shape. Young man, look at yourself in the mirror."

The light came on. Cargill, in spite of the words not knowing what to expect, stepped over to the mirror.

A Shadow image was reflected back at him.

"Oh, my lord!" he thought. He looked down at himself. He was a Shadow, too.

He began to feel the difference. His vision sharpened. He turned toward the mirror. It seemed now to be less substantial, as if most of the light beyond it were visible. In the next instant he was looking through the mirror. He stood on a height and his vision was Olympian. A speck in the distant sky beyond the now completely invisible pyramid touched his tension. His vision leaped to it. It was a bird, a hawk, wheeling in flight.

Astounded at the remarkable telescopic effect, he drew back into the room and looked at the floor. It half-dissolved before his eyes and then became as transparent as glass. He looked down at the floor below, down into the soil beneath. It was bright and dark brown, then gray stone, then brown-red soil, then a dark shale, then—it was harder to see. Some kind of clay, he decided finally. Below that he couldn't make it out at all. He drew his gaze back, conscious that there were depths he could not penetrate.

The voice said, "Now, we bring you back to normal. Please notice though that what counted was the direction of your attention. The general secret is vibration and visualization."

The mirror was visible again. The image of Morton Cargill was reflected back at him.

The voice said: "Do you wish to make any comments or ask any questions?"

Cargill hesitated; then he asked, "Is there a theory about the Shadow shape? What is your explanation for the way solid substance can be reduced to apparent insubstantialness?"

The other was silent; then he laughed softly and said: "I could, of course, say that matter does not really exist. This has been long understood."

Cargill nodded, abruptly feeling sardonic. Scientists had paid lip service to that notion in the Twentieth Century. And then, in their daily life, they acted as if matter were real. He wondered if he might now get closer to the world that he had explored in his—he kept thinking of it as a *dream*.

The voice was speaking again: "The reality here, however, is that we probably make the body more substantial, not less. This is so because we use energy from an outside source, and fit it so perfectly into the body flows that we have, in effect, additional life energy available. We have tested this at all potencies up to and including death, which of course can be induced by too much energy as well as by a reduction of what is there.

"The results of these tests were fascinating. As we raised the energy level, the person became progressively sane. Then there was a curious reversion, then an upward movement again, then down, then up—but with different phenomena at each level. The cyclic change occurred right up to where the insubstantiality began, seeming to follow this positive and negative pattern throughout. We had some dangerous reactions at the higher negative levels.

"If you can visualize a man of supreme intelligence who is wholly evil, you will have the picture. The first time we achieved such an effect, we were lucky. Thereafter, we anticipated and took precautions, but despite that, several times it was touch and go. Does that to some extent answer your questions?"

Cargill was silent, considering. Nothing that had been said conflicted basically with the strange ideas which he had had in his first dream. According to what he had *known* in the dream, outside energy was unnecessary. But if that were actually so, then these Shadows had not yet discovered the methods necessary to achieve that effortless state. He shook his head finally. "No questions at the moment," he said.

"Very well. Except for some minor conditioning you can now make yourself a Shadow at will, merely by thinking it so. The second door is now unlocked. It leads to a series of apartments. The ones that show a green light are unoccupied and you may select one of them as your own for the time being. I'll call you presently."

The apartment he entered was surprisingly large, five rooms and two baths. Cargill explored it hurriedly; he stopped only when he saw the phone. It was in a little alcove and it included a TV scanner and a viewing plate against the wall. On the lower right corner of the viewer—and it was that that interested him—was a series of small knobs. Above them was the word: DIRECTORY.

With fingers that trembled he first explored the mechanical process, then manipulated the three knobs that had the letters of the alphabet arranged on them. He set the first one for G, the next for R, the third and last for A. Then he pressed the switch.

A long list of names flashed on to the viewer: Granger, Granholm, Grannell, Grant . . .

There was no Grannis listed.

"But that's ridiculous," Cargill thought. "Now is the time for me to get hold of him before he can transmit the cue word to me." At the moment he could turn the equivalent of a mobile spit gun on Grannis before the man could suspect his intention or change into the protective Shadow shape. Surely he would be vulnerable in his human form. "I've got to find him," he told himself. "There must be some reason why he isn't listed. If I could only ask questions about that!"

There was a clock in the living room and it showed ten minutes after ten. That galvanized him. Suppose they had selected noon today for him to disconnect the pyramid switch.

He left the apartment hastily by an entrance that opened onto a winding street, a shopping center. The stores were crowded with shoppers and he had to stifle an impulse to go into one of the spacious buildings. He did pause to peer in at a window, but that merely emphasized the normalcy of the whole situation.

He hurried on. Although aware that he was a man with a deadly mission, he had no idea where to go to carry it out. He only knew that it must be done quickly. For a while he walked feverishly along quiet shady streets. Here in the residential area the houses were set well back behind flower and shrub gardens. Children played in most of the yards. At different times he saw both men and women working among the shrubs. Not once did he see a Shadow. It was a role and a condition they assumed for time travel and in case danger threatened. Agitatedly, Cargill wondered how quickly they could put on their protective cloaks of darkness.

Time and again he looked on the name plates for the name, Grannis. As the morning lengthened towards midday the virtual impossibility of his search being successful penetrated deeper. A man who was not even listed in the directory would not be locatable by a hasty street-to-street search in a city of more than a hundred thousand people.

He admitted defeat abruptly and hurried back toward his apartment. "I'll stay inside," he thought. "I won't answer the door. I won't answer the phone. That way no one can give me the cue."

He had the empty feeling that he had made a mistake in leaving the place at all. As he approached the square building, his watch, which he had set by the clock in the apartment, pointed at twenty minutes to twelve. Cargill began to perspire. He was surprised to notice that several hundred people were gathered in front of an entrance to one of the great round buildings. Cargill asked one of them, "What's happening?"

The stranger glanced at him with a good-natured smile. "We're waiting for the announcement," he said. "We received notice from the future of the results of an election held today and we're waiting for verification."

Cargill hurried on. So they had elections, did they? He felt cynical and critical until he thought: "From the future? But Lan Bruch said there wasn't any future." The fact that such an election pronouncement had taken place cast a further doubt upon the integrity of the personnel in the 7301 A.D. incident, and indeed upon the reality of the vision itself. However, he was still reluctant to admit that it hadn't happened. Perhaps, if he asked careful questions, he might learn what had occurred.

At last he reached his apartment. As he entered the door a voice from the phone alcove said to him mechanically, "You are to report at once to Office One, Building C. Grannis requests that you report to Office One, Building C. You are to report to Office . . ."

Swiftly, after the first shock, Cargill emerged from

his daze. "I'll practice being a Shadow," he thought grimly. "I'll superimpose the spit gun tube and then—"

It seemed to him that he couldn't escape the necessity of killing Grannis, in spite of somebody coming from the future to hold an election. Everything that had happened so far he had forced by his own actions. Even knowing of the paradox did not relieve him of responsibility until he personally had done what was required. As of now only he knew of the imminent catastrophe, personal as well as national. Across the land Tweener and Planiacs must be now tensing for their desperate roles.

Cargill walked forward, shut off the automatic repeating device on the phone and left his apartment. Outside he asked a passerby which was Building C. A few minutes later he was at his destination.

The man in Office One of Building C was a large pleasant-looking individual with a touch of gray in his hair. He seemed about sixty years of age. He did not ask Cargill to sit down but instead stood up. "I'm getting old," he said to Cargill. "In spite of all my shuttling around, in spite of having lived altogether about a thousand years, old age has finally caught up with me. I used to think that would never happen."

He chuckled. "I've been Grannis now for eighty-seven years, so I'm rather glad that someone has been selected to replace me. It's unusual for a newcomer to be chosen but the choice was made by the people of the future and they put your name up and urged an immediate election. And so"—he waved at the large room—"here it is."

He became business-like. "It won't take you long to learn your duties. Protector of the State—that's easy. To do that properly you've got to live periodically among the Tweeners. They're the ones that have to be watched. What I did was to marry a Tweener girl—

that's in addition to my Shadow wife, but she died four years ago for the last time."

He didn't explain that but went on, "I suggest you take a look at what the Tweeners are up to sometime soon." He finished. "Then of course you sign documents authorizing therapies. You have no veto power on that but"— he smiled—"you'll get onto it."

He held out his hand. "And now, before I go, any questions?"

18

"Grannis!" said Cargill at that point. His mind had been a receptive blank. Now he felt the intense flow of his own strength.

The old man was amused. "As a newcomer," he said, "you won't know about our history. Our first leader, and discoverer of the Shadow principle, was named Grannis, and we carried on using his name as a synonym for leader."

"Grannis!" Cargill repeated. He had a blinding vision of the truth, a mental picture of one man using the time energy, first to save his own life, then to prevent unnecessary war, finally to establish himself in the twenty-fourth century as the Grannis of the Shadows. He said tautly, "Will you tell me a little bit more about my duties?"

As he listened his mind soared so swiftly that only a part of the meaning came through. His body was warm with excitement. His thoughts were vague and roseate and at first he had no desire to establish any logical connection with reality. Now *he* was Grannis: it would be for him now to plan the Planiac attack on the

Tweeners and the Tweener attack on the Shadows. He would do that not because of any traitorous scheme but because it was the way things had already happened.

Unsteadily, he halted the wilder gyrations of his thoughts. Tensely, he recalled the way he had been taken back to the therapy room here in Shadow City and from there on to the Tweener capital. Why had that been necessary? How did that fit?

Why live over again a period of this age? All he had to do was come to the terminal center, enter Shadow City and be on hand for the only kind of election where the electorate could decide on an officeholder's capacity after his term.

There was, of course, the fact that Grannis had merely tried to control, under great difficulties, plots that were already in the making. As Grannis he would be forced to act according to Morton Cargill's knowledge of what had happened. As Cargill he had acted according to Grannis' interference. He paused, astounded. "Just a moment," he thought. "That doesn't make sense. We can't both act according to what the other did. That would make it a closed circle—"

The older man interrupted him as he reached this thought in his logical progression. "Any more questions?" he asked.

Cargill had to come back a long way, and he had at least one question. "How did the people of the future let you know that I should be selected?"

The other smiled cheerfully. "Their representative, Lan Bruch, brought us a complete record of the voting, and introduced your name. After the vote today, a computer compared his transcript with the data on our voting machines, and when they matched name for name, we did not doubt that we had an accurate report from the future. Naturally, his introduction of your name produced a situation unique in our history. We are all rather interested to see what the results will be."

Cargill was thinking: "Lan Bruch of unformed, incomplete Merlica is grimly fighting to make himself real. But where does that leave the Shadows?" Not for the first time, it occurred to him that these Shadow supermen, despite their good will, didn't have more than a partial understanding of the energies they had tamed. Perhaps their concentration on the positive side of things would prove unwise. They were trying to live without boundaries, but perhaps that represented a fine balance between the positive and the negative, between right and wrong, between cause and effect, responsibility and no responsibility.

Of one thing there seemed no doubt. In this affair they were being taken advantage of. His thought poised there. He had been so intent that he had not noticed that fantasy had become reality. "Lan Bruch?" he asked aloud. *"Lan Bruch?"*

The older man said something which Cargill did not hear. He thought that if Lan Bruch had actually come from the future, *then that part of his dream was real.* It was the first verification, and therefore its importance could hardly be overestimated. In one jump what had happened became an incident, an event in space-time— well, somewhere. He had to remember that the space-time continuum of Merlica did not yet exist. Merlica would not become finally possible until the Tweeners won in their attack.

The realization chilled Cargill. For everything was moving in that direction, moving towards the achievement of that purpose. And yet it was still as true as ever that the destruction of Shadow City was intrinsically wrong. But the groundwork had been laid: at the critical moment in the history of the Shadow-Tweener age, Morton Cargill, hypnotized slave of the

Tweeners, occupied a position in Shadow City from which he could sally forth unchallenged to perform his act of treachery. All that was needed was the signal.

His predecessor was speaking: "I see it's half past twelve. I'll leave you to familiarize yourself with the office. You've got assistants in the outer room. Don't hesitate to use them."

Once more he held out his hand. This time Cargill shook it, saying: "I may need further advice. Visit me some time, will you?"

Because the older man was turning away, Cargill did not see the effect of his own words on him. *"Visit me some time!"*—the signal, that phrase that was to cue him to throw the pyramid switch. And he had given it to himself.

After the other had gone, Cargill slumped into a chair. Presently he felt a grudging admiration: clever idea, having him give himself the cue. It couldn't fail that way. Tricky thing, the human mind. How cunningly he had worked the phrase into an ordinary conversation. Presently Cargill roused himself. "I've got just over eleven hours," he thought. "The attack is obviously scheduled for midnight."

He stood up, remembering what the voice had told him, when he had first been transported from the cocktail bar in Los Angeles, 1954: that the body reacted with final positivity only to the impact of real events. The cue to disengage the pyramid switch had been given him. He knew his time limit. He knew the real event.

There remained one item: how had the Shadow therapists reacted to the disappearance of Morton Cargill from their therapy room two months ago? There must be a record of the incident. It would be here in one of the files of the Grannis.

He found the record almost at once. With a pale face Cargill read the notation under his name:

Morton Cargill, 1954. Recommended therapy: "To be killed in the presence of Betty Lane." Disposition: "Therapy executed at 9:40 A.M." Comments: "Subject seemed unusually calm at time of death."

That was all there was. Apparently, the process was so automatic that the everyday details were left out. Only the bare simple facts were permanently recorded.

Morton Cargill, despite all his frantic maneuverings, had somehow landed back in the therapy room and, without the Shadows even being aware of his wanderings, had at his proper time been given the prescribed treatment. There was no mention of what had been done with the body.

Cargill emerged slowly from his profound depression. "I don't believe it," he told himself. "Surely, as Grannis, I could have faked that report."

He read it again. Seeing that it was signed by two names in addition to his own and stamped with an official seal shook him a little, but stubbornly he held to his conviction. Besides, for all he knew, the death scene might be a thousand years in the future. These Shadows, with their tremendous understanding of life processes, had created the environment for just such a paradox.

The possibility definitely cheered him. He looked around the spacious office. He walked over and glanced out of a window that overlooked the lovely mountain city. For a moment then he was dazzled. He was the Grannis of the Shadow people. He could move through all the past ages of man at will. "And all I've got to do," he thought, "is make sure that everything happens as I know it happened."

Hastily he prepared for the paradox. First he changed himself into a Shadow and back again several times. Finally, as a Shadow he stood thinking, "I want to go back to—" He named the destination mentally. He waited but nothing happened. Startled, he refused to accept the defeat.

"I must be using the wrong technique," he told himself. The trouble was, what could be the right one? He remembered what the Shadow instructor had said about vibration and visualization.

He changed from the Shadow shape and thought, "What basic vibration can I use as a measure?" The only one he could remember was middle C on the musical scale. He hummed the C softly as he figured out on paper how many middle C vibrations there were in a day.

He changed back to the Shadow shape, visualized his destination again. Then he hummed middle C— and thought the number of vibrations.

He felt an indescribable tingle.

So, two hours before the volor-powered floater with Morton Cargill aboard left the Tweener capital for Shadow City, another Morton Cargill contacted Withrow. As a result, half an hour after the first Cargill was on his way and before any real counter-action could take effect, the Tweener revolution was launched.

The complete surprise achieved a virtually bloodless victory nearly ten hours ahead of schedule. The cue words, which were to have been sent to him to disconnect the pyramid switch, would never take effect.

Then Shadow Grannis-Cargill headed back in time to the floater on which Lela Bouvy and another Morton Cargill were trapped. Once inside the floater he transferred the "earlier" Cargill to the glass-walled therapy room in Shadow City, where presently Ann Reece would rescue him for the second time. As Grannis he returned immediately to the floater. Ignoring the cringing Lela he walked through to the engine room. After the training he had received he needed only one glance at the drive tube to notice that the light-focusing lens had been jarred out of position. He reached in with Shadow fingers and adjusted it. The floater started to rise immediately as normal energy-flow was resumed.

Once Lela was safe, he moved back in time and visited Carmean on the night that Lela and Morton Cargill escaped in Carmean's floater. By making casual references to previous meetings he found from Carmean when and where they had taken place. He began to keep a diary of his movements, then thought in an anguish of self-annoyance, "Why, of course, this very diary will be up there in the future. I'd have put it where it would be easy to find."

Back in Shadow City, he located it in the top drawer of Grannis' desk. The list was there, complete with names, places and actions taken.

The job done, he returned to Office One, Building C, Shadow City. It was one minute after his previous departure. The time was 1:01 P.M. Because of the time paradox, only a few hours had gone by in Shadow City since he had first arrived at the terminal center.

At five minutes after one the phone rang. It was the instructor who had given him Shadow training. "If you will come to cubicle eleven," he instructed Cargill, "we will discuss further training. There isn't much but still it is a part of our pattern."

Cargill walked over to the cubicle, thinking, "If only I could ask a question about that death scene in such a way that I wouldn't give myself away." He had tried to imagine just how he might be present when the therapy was executed but he rejected the idea. There might be such a thing as straining a paradox to the point where it wouldn't work.

As soon as he had entered cubicle eleven the light went out and the disembodied voice spoke out of the air in front of him. "Long ago, when we first discovered the processes involved, we decided that every Shadow must go through the experiences of death and, of course, revival. The reason for this is the universal fear of death. When a person actually goes through death and is brought back to life the associative terror, except in rare cases, is gone forever. The process of dying also has other effects on the system. Particularly, it breaks forever certain types of tensions. For this latter reason we do not hesitate to recommend it as a therapy for people we bring out of the past in our inter-time psychological work—"

"What's that?" Cargill thought at that point. "What did you say?" But he did not utter the startled questions out loud.

The instructor continued, "We always revive the therapy patient after he and the complaining party are convinced on the action level that death has indeed taken place, though the complainant is never aware of the resurrection. Many of these latter are morally shocked by what has happened, but we use the million tube to persuade them that justice has been done. And with that combination, and that only, the effect we want is achieved."

Cargill said slowly, "This death experience—can the same person undergo it several times without being harmed?"

"Very few Shadows," was the reply, "would live to be a thousand years old if that were not true. You cannot imagine the number of accidents that take place despite all precautions." He finished with a hint of irony in his tone, "We do not, however, recommend the death experience more than a dozen times. The cells begin to remember the process."

Cargill hesitated. "There's another thing that's been bothering me. Can I go into my own future?"

"No. Only a pattern which has already occurred can be repeated by the body. For you to go into the future from here would require that somebody from the future pull you 'up.' The pattern would then be established, and you could operate from that particular future into the past."

Cargill didn't argue against the limitations. His reason for asking had to do with his experience with Lan Bruch. He was certain now that in some way Lan Bruch had drawn him into the future that was Merlica. The rest of the "happenings" seemed to be more in the nature of a stirring-up of long-buried memory.

He didn't want anything like that to happen here, didn't want any random intrusion of extra-sensory phenomena to interfere with his Shadow training. The question was, however, how would he avoid it? If there were any kind of *separation* at death, then he, with his previous experiences, would be aware of it and would afterwards remember.

Cargill said slowly: "When should I have this death experience?"

"That's up to you. You can take it now or wait for an accidental death. The point is *you* must decide."

Cargill hesitated. The idea of dying right now startled him. And, besides, he could already think of several things he ought to accomplish first. It was also possible that he could disassociate his "death" from Betty Lane's therapy and instead consider it as part of his necessary training, and get it over with.

"I'll wait," he said finally.

"Very well," said the voice; "call me when you're ready."

There was a click and the door unlocked.

Cargill wasted no time. He had thought of several additional things he ought to do before he could be certain he was in this age to stay.

There was, for instance, that very first time when Ann Reece had brought Captain Morton Cargill, newly arrived from the twentieth century, to a marble room where he had had an opportunity to see and be seen by the Shadow Grannis. The reason for contact had been obscure. Now, it was suddenly clear. "Of course," he thought, "it was important that Cargill see a Shadow. Besides that was the simplest way to get back the transport instrument that had to be loaned to Ann so that she could make the rescue."

And there was the matter of the false notions the Tweeners and Planiacs had had about what the Shadows could and could not do. Some of that, of course, was due to their own ignorance, but Grannis must have confirmed their ideas with deliberate intent to deceive. And finally there was the fact that there had been previous getaways. It seemed incredible, now, that some Tweeners and Planiacs had escaped by themselves. Grannis must have helped them. Why? In order to establish among Planiacs the reality of the existence of such people, so that when Morton Cargill came along, his identity as a getaway would be taken for granted.

Cargill sighed. The task of establishing oneself in the future was an intricate one, involving many details.

But he carried these out, one by one. . . .

Later, heading for the therapy room in Shadow City, he was willing at last to receive the treatment that had once seemed so incredible. Apparently, going through the act of dying would be a minor experience to go through. It was Betty Lane, the observer, who would have the shock; he anticipated none. Nevertheless, there was one question in Cargill's mind as he waited in his half of the double apartment for the executioner to come for him. The question concerned Lan Bruch, of far Merlica.

The man had been at the point of telling him what he, Cargill, must do so that the Tweeners would win. It was strange that the entire Merlica scene had faded at the precise moment when those words were spoken.

The questions was, had he, in fact, heard the words? Was it possible that he knew what the method was by which the Tweeners could win? Could all that he had done to insure that the Tweeners did *not* win be undone at this late stage by some unexpected event?

Cargill assured himself that no change was likely. But as the voice of the "therapist" projected into the air near his head, Cargill thought: "If I can recall how those geometric designs looked, maybe I can get close enough to Merlica to remember exactly what Lan Bruch said."

19

Eerily, Cargill appeared to be detached from his real self and able to watch the scene below him. And yet, in a paradoxical fashion, he was still part of it. He would have liked to withdraw the billions of energy flows that connected him with the inanimate thing down there. But he knew the body wasn't as yet really dead, although the major motion had ceased. The heart, the lungs, all the organs had stopped functioning.

The holding effect of the body was highly disturbing because there was some place *he* was supposed to go. He realized that this experience was different than others he had had. In the past he had not questioned the need to go, had not questioned where he should go, had simply gone there. Now, he thought: "Why *should* I go anywhere?"

And that was, indeed, a new idea. There was confidence in it: as a concept, not as an emotion. Curiously, he observed the body that had been Morton Cargill; dispassionately, he watched what was being done. He directed a flow through the wall toward the energy tube that had effected the body's death, and was now forcing alterations. Some of the alterations interfered with the long-established all-wave flow that interrelated him with the space-time-energy complex below, which he suddenly realized was just a part of his own universe. The interference was interesting in that it seemed to be aimed at enturbulated areas, which looked black from where he was.

As the tube did its work, the disturbed flow in the area under attack slowly took on a whitish hue. Interested, Cargill looked around for black areas, and, finding some outside of the body somewhat to his left, turned them white, also. He was still busily engaged in turning even more distant black spots white when he remembered the geometric design that had led him to the lake and the statue, and to Merlica. He had come upon Merlica as if by chance, he recalled. The "fabric" of the design had moved, as if someone other than he himself were controlling it. He conjured it up, to one side, near him. And there was the movement! The fabric shook and twisted, and would not hold still.

Somehow, he knew exactly what to do. He picked first a small area of the design, blotted out the rest, and exaggerated all of the automatic movements of the tiny area, periodically trying to hold it still. On his third try he held it completely motionless without effort.

Immediately, he brought the entire design into view and began to exaggerate the automatic motions in the larger area. And this, also, he strove every few moments to hold still.

It took four tries. Then he succeeded.

"What have I accomplished?" he wondered.

He was still somehow hovering above the dead body of Morton Cargill, above the white-faced descendant of Marie Chanette. He looked around and saw that several dozen energy flows came out of the distance, and connected to the body. He knew, without thinking about it, that their sources were far away in space-time.

Cargill reached down firmly with a complex flow of his own and disconnected the intruding "lines," one by one. The first one had a startled thought behind it. It was the thought of Lan Bruch, saying: "He's defeated us." The second line went down, and a thought came along it, which stated: "I doubt if the cities of space should interfere."

The messages that came along the other lines were more difficult to translate into words, but the meaning of the thoughts was that such disconnection had never occurred before. Laughter came along one of the lines. There was no humor in it, but there was sardonic understanding. The meaning of the laughter and of the understanding came to Cargill. They implied that he had learned some of the rules of the game, and therefore had become a sub-player, at least.

Somewhere, a strong voice said: "Let's change the rules of that universe."

The answer echoed along the same line: "He's already making his own rules."

"That," was the reply, "is the quickest way to become a broken piece."

Cargill thought grimly: "So Lan Bruch thinks I've defeated him. Good." Then he wouldn't need to know what the man had said. That control was broken at an energy level.

Cargill thought tensely: *"There isn't really anybody else in my universe. All those thoughts are my own. I'm playing this game, and I'm all the pieces, and all the players, and I'm the—"*

He couldn't quite let that last idea come to full flowering.

He made the effort not to know what he had thought. He made an agreement with himself that he would remember. He reinforced those rules of the game that made it necessary for him to hide the memory from himself. He considered several methods by which he could punish himself for all future time for having even momentarily revealed—what?

He couldn't remember.

He opened his eyes and looked up at the two Shadows who had performed the therapy. One of them walked away almost immediately. The other gazed down at Cargill with inscrutable, dull eyes, and then made an unmistakable gesture: Sit up!

As he obeyed, he realized the difference within himself. He felt refreshed and energized, wonderfully alert and alive. The million-tube had probably been used on him to educate him, to explain why he passed through this experience. For he knew with a sharper understanding that he had been relaxed while Betty Lane had had the equivalent of a cathartic experience.

Old, old was that pattern. Punishment is known among animals and when there is none, neurosis strikes as deeply into the mind of the beast as any comparable situation in man. A bull elephant, nursing along his females, is attacked by a larger bull and is driven into the jungle. The injustice of it tears him to pieces, and after a time a dangerous rogue elephant roams the forest. There was a hell before heaven was thought of. Once people were hanged for stealing a shilling—until twenty-five cents ceased to be an important sum. Morality changed, of course. The crime of one generation was common practice in the next and so a thousand easements came automatically to the tensed descendants of people who did not have the satisfaction of catharsis. But there were eternal verities. Murder would be paid for by someone. Gross obscenities left their impress on the protoplasm. Revolutions and wars conducted without regard for the humanities—ah, but how they would be paid for! Disaster shocked the universe and the impulse went on and on. The shock waves of the collapse of vanished empires continued for ages.

The victim gains catharsis when the thief is captured and imprisoned. The prisoner, his guilt expiated by his imprisonment, also gains easement. . . . There was only one thing wrong with that. As Cargill sat up, relaxed and free, he realized for the first time that there was still another thing he must do.

This "prisoner" had not yet committed the crime which would make it possible for Morton Cargill to come to the twenty-fourth century.

It was 1953. A Shadow moved along a street of Los Angeles. It took a little while to locate the exact cocktail bar. He couldn't remember clearly where he had been that night at the beginning of the chain of events. Suddenly, however, he saw the sign that jarred his memory: ELBOW ROOM. A glance through the wall showed him Morton Cargill inside. He caught no sight of Marie Chanette.

That puzzled Shadow Grannis-Cargill. He stepped back into the darkness of a doorway across the street from the bar and for the first time seriously considered what he was about to do. He realized that in the back of his mind all this time he had deliberately forgotten the incident. Somehow he had known that sooner or later he would have to come to the twentieth century and make sure that everything happened *as it had happened*. He had to be certain that Marie Chanette did indeed die.

Cargill thought shakily, "Am I really going to let her be killed, knowing that I can stop it at any time up to the actual moment of the accident?"

Having put the question so sharply he had a sense of a desperate crisis. It had to be done, he argued wit

himself. If he faltered now everything might be disar-
ranged. He had been warned about trying to alter
events. Alteration required a closed circle of occur-
rences. Single changes could be made over a great
period of time, but tests carried out by teams of Shadows had established that objects could be moved without apparent dislocation. Human beings, and other life
forms, could be transferred from one place to another,
or from one time period to the past or future. But one
could not, must not, and should not interfere with a life
cycle that was known to have ended. After a man
had been dead hundreds of years, or scores, or long
enough to decompose, no interference should be attempted.

Marie Chanette was known to have died. The record
of her death had already resulted in a diagnosis which
had caused Morton Cargill to have a series of experiences. More important, she was the first event in
what he was endeavoring to make a complete cycle of
events where everything fitted logically.

Grannis-Cargill stood in the dim light and realized
unhappily that he was not really thinking logically
about the matter. After all, what could happen? So
many changes had already taken place. It seemed
ridiculous that one more would matter. The Shadow
experimenters were simply being careful.

He could imagine that before any really scientific
investigation had been made, things had happened
which would now be frowned upon by the experts.
. . . Well, maybe that wasn't quite true. The entire
Shadow phenomenon must always have been carried on
by scientists. No one else would have had the opportunity.

He was still undecided when the drunken Lieutenant
Cargill, still yet to return from service overseas a cap-

tain, staggered to his feet and came out of the bar into the darkness.

But where was the girl?

The Shadow Grannis-Cargill had a sudden flash of insight. In abrupt excitement he projected himself to the scene of the accident. He saw the wrecked car against a tree almost immediately. Inside was Marie Chanette. He examined her. Judging from her condition she had been dead nearly an hour.

"I didn't do it," said Grannis-Cargill aloud into the night. "I never even met the girl. She had the accident all by herself."

He was genuinely amazed. It was a totally unexpected outcome. It made complicated what he must do now: he had to make certain that everything occurred exactly as up to now he himself had believed.

The "earlier" Cargill must be convinced that he was partly responsible for the death of Marie Chanette. Why Marie had been selected at all, where she fitted in, seemed to grow more obscure by the minute.

Reluctant, and yet relieved by what he had discovered of his own innocence, he hastened back to where Lieutenant Cargill was standing, swaying. The drunk Cargill was unaware of the being who hovered behind him, directing on him the power of a million-tube. Without his being aware of it, the belief was impressed on his mind that at this moment he was meeting Marie Chanette.

The hallucination firmly established, Grannis-Cargill was about to transport the earlier Cargill to the wreck when he thought: "All I've got to do is go back an hour and a half in time and I can save Marie Chanette's life."

Suddenly, he said aloud, "No!"

It was not really a rejection, he realized wretchedly. He tried to argue with himself. "If I once get started on a thing like this, I could spend the rest of my life just preventing accidents."

"Besides," he reasoned, "she did it herself. I'm not responsible in any way." Abruptly he realized he was not convincing himself. General truths simply did not apply. Marie Chanette was one woman in the vast universe, one bewildered human being on the drift of time. In the moment before her death she must have cried out in sudden agonized awareness of her fate.

Shadow Grannis-Cargill made his choice: life for Marie Chanette. He stood grimly a few minutes later, watching her car come towards the scene of the accident.

He noted the direction from which she was coming, went back in time and space—and so by jumps traced her to the point where she came out of a night club accompanied by a soldier. The two were quarreling bitterly in drunken fashion. Cargill decided not to wait. Before the girl could get into her car he transported her to her bedroom.

Then he returned to what would normally have been the time and the scene of the accident. "I'll wait here till the moment for it is past," he decided.

The instant arrived when, earlier, Marie Chanette would have died.

In space-time, an energy thread "broke." In a certain area, the illusion that was space collapsed. It instantly ceased to *have* energy flow, and so instantly ceased to be a part of the universe of *doing*. Facsimiles of "dead" space automatically mocked-up in the disorganized area, and moment by moment were unmocked by the violence of the energy flows that poured in upon them. Several times, facsimiles of space, that were almost like what had been destroyed, held against the chaos for a measurable time in terms of billionths of seconds.

The space-time continuum in its grandeur had just about one second of existence left to it.

Cargill was already dead. At the very split-instant of the first "break," his body had all the space pulled out of it, and it ceased to be except as a body facsimile of something that continued to think like Cargill, and had Cargill's memories, and was Cargill in the sense that the entire body is the cell, and whole is the part.

The being who had for thirty-odd years been Morton Cargill looked out upon *the* universe with his thousands of perceptions. What had happened this time was clearly different. Somehow, his awareness had been stirred, and he knew who he was.

Mirror-wise, he reflected the entire material universe, reflected all universe, reflected First Cause, reflected *being*. He glanced back over the seventy trillion years of that mirror-picture, and saw where he had agreed to participate in the Game of the Material Universe.

And why!

The timeless static that had been Morton Cargill decided to renew the agreement; and the question was, should it be done through a change of the rules of the Game, or by adherence to them?

He did a magical thing. He mocked up the entire material universe, and changed the rules one by one, and two by two, and in intricate combinations. And then, he unmocked that universe, and mocked up a duplicate of the material universe. He put Marie Chanette into various positions, and had her die in consecutive moments, each time observing the effect on the mirror image that reflected in the static that was himself.

He saw that the illusion of life could be maintained *only* by having. And that implicit in having was losing. All the life-discards—like the lake and the statue—were meaningless developments because that one vital fact had not been known—then.

Marie Chanette must die.

But an attempt should be made to have her contact reality.

The static, in its mirror wisdom, reflecting as it did thought, magic, illusion and beauty, created a small amount of space.

The broken energy thread re-fused. A series of flows started. Dazed, Marie Chanette shook her head and climbed into her car. What puzzled her was the momentary conviction that she had been in her own bedroom. She was so intent on the thought that she forgot the soldier and drove away even as he was stumbling around to the other side to get in.

Grimly, Shadow Grannis-Cargill waited for the crash. When it was over, he transported the earlier Cargill to the wrecked car and put him into the seat beside Marie Chanette. He took the pictures that would "later"—in 1954—shock Captain Cargill.

He waited there, then, until the terrible tensions in him let up, waited till he could think, "I've broken through the barriers of life and death. The whole sidereal universe is open to me now that I know the truth."

Satisfied, he returned to Shadow City. The cycle was complete.